ALSO BY MITALI PERKINS

Monsoon Summer
The Not-So-Star-Spangled Life of Sunita Sen
Rickshaw Girl
Secret Keeper

FIRST DAUGHTER NOVELS

White House Rules
Extreme American Makeover

MITALI PERKINS

BAMBOO PEOPLE

a novel

ᴉᴪᴉ Charlesbridge

First paperback edition 2012
Copyright © 2010 by Mitali Perkins

Published by Charlesbridge
85 Main Street
Watertown, MA 02472
(617) 926-0329
www.charlesbridge.com

Library of Congress Cataloging-in-Publication Data

Perkins, Mitali.
  Bamboo people / Mitali Perkins.
    p. cm.
  Summary: Two Burmese boys, one a Karenni refugee and the other the son of
an imprisoned Burmese doctor, meet in the jungle and in order to survive
they must learn to trust each other.
  ISBN 978-1-58089-328-2 (reinforced for library use)
  ISBN 978-1-58089-329-9 (softcover)
1. Burma—Juvenile fiction. [1. Burma—Fiction. 2. Survival—Fiction.] I.Title.
PZ7.P4315Bam 2010
[Fic]—dc22   2009005495

Printed in the United States of America
(hc) 10 9 8 7 6 5 4 3
(sc) 10 9 8 7 6 5 4 3

Display type hand-lettered by Carol Chu and text type set in Goudy
Printed and bound August 2013 by Worzalla Publishing Company
    in Stevens Point, Wisconsin, USA
Production supervision by Brian G. Walker
Designed by Susan Mallory Sherman, with decorations by Carol Chu

For Burmese and Karenni young people

PART ONE

CHIKO

1

Teachers wanted. Applicants must take examination in person. Salaries start at—

"Chiko, come inside!" Mother calls through the screen door, her voice low and urgent.

On the road behind our house, horns toot, sirens blare, and bicycle rickshaws crowd the streets. A high cement wall and a barrier of bamboo muffle the noise, making our garden seem as private as a monastery. But it isn't. I could be spotted from the houses nearby, and spies are everywhere. They would betray even an old neighbor for extra ration cards.

3

I scan the rest of the announcement quickly, my heart racing.

"Chiko! *Now!*" Mother startles the flock of green parakeets perched on the birdbath, and they fly away.

I fold the newspaper around A *Tale of Two Cities* and head for the house. I want to tell Mother about the call for teachers in the paper, but it seems like she's getting more anxious by the day. So am I, even though I wish I didn't have to admit that. I'm tired of hiding, of worrying, and worst of all, of remembering again and again the day the soldiers came for Father. Remembering how I've failed him.

"You shouldn't be reading out there," Mother tells me, peering out through the screen after latching the door behind me.

I take a deep breath and push my glasses back. It's now or never. "No harm in reading the government newspaper. There's a notice—"

But she's not listening. "We'll talk about that later, Chiko. How could you take one of your father's books outside? Do you want to end up in prison, too?"

She's right—I shouldn't have brought the book out there. The government gets suspicious when a Burmese boy reads English books. But I don't answer her questions. What can I say? That it already feels like I'm in prison? I take the novel out of the newspaper. The worn cloth cover is still warm from the sunshine. "Read widely,

Chiko," Father used to say. "Great doctors must understand human nature in order to heal."

"Hide it right now, Chiko," Mother says sharply. "Wait. Let me draw the blinds."

The dim room grows even darker. I reach behind the large painting of a white elephant, and we hear the familiar click. The painting swings open silently, like a well-oiled door. Hidden behind it is the cabinet Father built to conceal his battered black medical bag, books, and papers.

The books are in the same order as he left them, and I slip *A Tale of Two Cities* into place. There are a dozen medical and college textbooks, but we also own the complete works of Shakespeare, a book about Buddha's teachings, the Christian Holy Bible, a few slim volumes of British poetry, an illustrated Oxford dictionary, some Burmese books (like the Jakata tales and verses by Thakin Kodaw Hmaing and Tin Moe), novels by Indian and Russian writers like Rabindranath Tagore and Fyodor Dostoevsky, *The Arabian Nights*, and a set of books by Charles Dickens. These are our family treasures—faded, tattered, and well read.

I'm one of the few boys in town who can read and write in Burmese and English. It's only because of Father. Schools around here close down so often it's hard to learn, but I studied at home.

Father's favorite books explain the secrets and

mysteries of the human body, from bones to blood to cells to nerves. I always loved stories the best—books about heroes and quests and adventures, books where everything turns out fine in the end. I tried to pretend to be interested in science, but Father wasn't fooled; he used the novels as prizes after we studied science.

It's no use remembering the good times we had. I think I miss the sound of him the most. His voice— reading, talking, or laughing—steadied the house like a heartbeat. These days I only hear the conversation of Mother and her friends. If this keeps up, my own voice might reverse itself and start sounding high and sweet again.

I remember the last time I heard Father speak—almost four months ago. "Take care of your mother, Chiko!" he shouted as six or seven army officers shoved him into a van.

"I will, Father!" I answered, hoping he heard.

But have I kept that promise? No! All I've done is hide, and that's not good enough with our money running out. And it's terrible to go without news of him. The same thought keeps both Mother and me awake at night, even though we never say it to each other. *Is he alive?*

2

"We can talk after you eat lunch, Chiko," Mother urges, pushing a chair to the table. "It's getting late. Daw Widow and Lei will be coming for tea. Daw Widow says she has some something important to tell us."

Daw Widow is our next-door neighbor. She's offered a reward for any information about Father's arrest. It's impossible to get real news, but rumors float through the streets. Bicycle rickshaw passengers whisper to one another, forgetting that drivers with sharp ears pedal the cycles.

That's how Daw Widow discovered why Father was arrested. Someone had spotted him when he crept out from our house at night to treat a patient—an "enemy of the state," a leader of the freedom and democracy movement. They'd charged Father as a traitor to the government for providing money and information along with medical care. Even though we don't know where he's imprisoned, or even if he's still alive, we have to send money to the government every month to pay for his food.

Mother sets a covered plate before me. "Daw Widow has been scolding me about how skinny you're getting," she says. "Before I know it, she'll be checking my pantry and giving me cooking lessons again."

The familiar dimple in Mother's left cheek deepens. Father used to say that he tumbled into it when he first saw her and never climbed out. But lately a pattern of creases and wrinkles is starting to hide it. "She must like your cooking, Mother," I say. "She always eats seconds when she's here, and sometimes thirds, if there's enough."

Still smiling, Mother hurries to the kitchen to slice me a lime. I lift the cover off the plate and see *ngapi*, the dried and fermented shrimp paste we eat with every meal; rice; and a few chunks of chicken floating in a pale, weak curry. I've been trying to get Mother to eat more by having her eat first. She's even thinner than I am, but she hides it under the loose folds of her sarong. I hunt and count pieces of chicken—she hasn't taken any meat at all. I'm going to have to change my strategy and eat before she does so I can leave her most of the meat.

Mother returns with three juicy, green wedges, so I squeeze lime over my food and start eating. I want to finish before our guests arrive because I've started feeling uncomfortable eating in front of Lei. With those dark eyes watching me, I feel like a tiger, tearing and chewing away at my dinner—a big cat predator in square-rimmed glasses.

After I'm done, Mother clears the table and brings out her mending. The look on her face tells me she's hoping I won't bring up the newspaper announcement. Father's voice in my mind reminds me to study, so I sigh, open the cabinet again, and take out a calculus book.

It's impossible to concentrate today. After pretending for a while, I glance at Mother's face. Time's running out—the interview for teachers is at four o'clock. I'll have to leave soon if I want to make it. Besides, Daw Widow will be here shortly, and she'll probably put up an even bigger fight than Mother to stop me.

Now or never, Chiko, I tell myself, taking off my glasses and rubbing my eyes. "Mother."

The needle keeps going, but she's frowning.

"Mother." I try again.

She looks up. "All right, Chiko. What was in the paper?"

"The government wants to hire teachers. They're giving an exam this afternoon. I want to take it."

"And you believe them?"

"It *might* be true. And if I pass the test, they'll hire me. The salary's small, but—"

Mother flings aside her sewing and stands up. "You are *not* leaving this home, Chiko. Young men are disappearing every day. Just last week We-Min's son was at the market when soldiers dragged him away to join the army. And *his* father's still at home."

She's right. It could be dangerous for me out there. And the notice in the paper could be a lie. But I can't live like this any longer, cowering inside this house while Mother gets thinner and our money runs out. I made a promise; I have to try to keep it.

"Times are changing," I tell her. "Daw Widow told us about the rumors that some of the prisoners might be set free. This job—if it's real—might pay enough for us to keep taking care of Father until he's released."

Mother has already sold her jewelry and our extra clothes. The toaster, the fan, the radio, and even most of the pots and pans are gone. Last month she even sold some of Father's medical equipment, knowing that he'd want us to eat. All we have left are our family treasures, hidden in that cabinet behind the white elephant.

"We're going to have to sell the books," I say, even though I know what Mother's reaction will be.

"No! Your father brought those back from England before we were married. Selling them is like . . ."

It's my turn to stand up. "Like what, Mother? Like admitting that Father might not come back? Well, what if he doesn't? Our money's gone!"

"Your father *will* come back, young man!" She steadies her voice. "He's alive; I can feel his heart beating inside mine."

I press my lips together to keep more disrespectful words from pouring out. Superstitions and old wives' tales won't help Father survive; we've heard stories about how they treat "enemies of the state."

"I know it's hard for you to hide like this, my son," Mother continues. "Won't you change your mind and join the temple?"

The suggestion is tempting, and she knows it. Soldiers don't harass monks, and boys my age often serve the temple for a year or two. But I can't become a monk, not with Father's last words to take care of Mother ringing in my ears, mind, and heart. Not with the memory of me doing nothing while they dragged him away.

"No, Mother. The temple won't pay me a salary."

"I can find sewing work here and there," says Mother. "And you'd be safe, Chiko."

That word triggers something inside me. "Safe!" I shoot it at her like a bullet, and she flinches. "Maybe I'm not supposed to be safe. We're behind in the rent and running out of food. And what am I doing about it?"

Mother holds up one hand, palm facing me. "Stop!"

she says, and her voice is stern. "They've taken my husband. I don't intend to hand over my son."

Somebody raps on the door, and we both jump.

"Who is it?" Mother calls, her voice trembling.

The day the soldiers arrested Father, the three of us were arguing about my going away. Father wanted me to apply to colleges in England. He still has friends there, friends who could help get me into university. Mother, of course, didn't want me to go, but she hates that her last words to Father were angry ones.

I take her hand. If the army *is* here to take me, I don't want our final moments to bring any more crying in the night. "Speak up!" I call, even though my stomach is clenched like a fist. "Who's there?"

3

The hinges of the front door creak, and a rusty voice calls out, "Wei-Lin! I heard that boy of yours shouting from my kitchen. *And* I saw him reading a book. *Outside*."

It's only Daw Widow. Mother lets go of my hand. Quickly I stand up straight and push up my glasses. Lei enters the house behind her mother, looking like an orchid in her slim green sarong. Her purple silk blouse seems to carry the sunlight into our house.

Daw Widow stays in front of her, blocking my

view, hands on her hips. "What's the fight about this time?"

Mother manages a smile. "The boy wants to leave, Ah-Ma." My mother is always proper, never forgetting to address Daw Widow as her older sister. "He wants to prove something, I think. That he can be as brave as Joon was—is, I mean."

We're quiet, pretending not to notice her slip of the tongue. Then Daw Widow advances, one finger jabbing the air in front of my face. "So you want to go to college, do you? Let me tell you something—you don't learn to be a doctor from books," she says. She pokes the calculus book I'm using as a shield. "Your father didn't, either. I never thought much of his fancy foreign education, anyway. The knowledge they stuffed into his head from these books didn't make him the finest doctor in Burma. He was a healer even before he went away. The heavens gave him a special gift."

I always feel like groaning when Mother or Daw Widow brings up this old village belief. Father's medical skills a gift from heaven? Hah! I've seen his detailed, neat lecture notes; reviewed his stellar examination records; watched him do research for hours. Hard work and a clever mind—those are the keys to the medical profession, not some magical healing touch. Besides, why does everyone assume I want to be a doctor, anyway? I don't

14

want to deal with blood and broken bones. Lei might be the only one who knows my distaste for medicine, and only because I confessed it to her once when we were alone.

"No use getting that know-it-all look on your face," Daw Widow scolds, her sharp eyes studying my expression. "Your father had a gift, I tell you. There was something in his face that made people feel better *before* he gave them any of those Western medicines. A glow, or a light in his eyes. When he left, he took a patient's worries and fears away in that black bag of his."

"I know just what you mean," Mother chimes in. "Joon's old medical professor came for tea last week. When he smiled and told me Joon would be well, I believed him. He left such a feeling of peace behind."

I shrug, remembering how the old man's lined features seemed to brighten as he looked at Mother. It was nighttime when he visited, and the flickering kerosene lamp cast a strange pattern of light onto our faces. But I'm tired of old wives' tales and fears. It's time for some truth telling. "I don't want to become a doctor," I announce. "I want to be a teacher."

"Teach?" Daw Widow asks. "Your father wanted you to be a doctor, young man."

"I know. But he'd be glad if I chose to be a teacher."

Daw Widow snorts. "Anyway, you're too young."

"That's what I've been trying to tell him," Mother says. Shaking her head, she heads into the kitchen to get the tea.

"No snacks for us today, Wei-Lin, dear," Daw Widow calls in the direction of the kitchen. "Lei and I had a big lunch."

Unlike Mother, Daw Widow has a steady source of income. Her husband was a postal officer before he died, and a small government pension still comes every month.

I pull out two chairs. After her mother is seated, Lei gathers the folds of her sarong and sits down. I smell the faint, clean scent of soap on her skin and fight the urge to touch the shining curtain of hair that swings across her shoulders.

She looks up. "Do you have time to teach *me* today? It's been a while since you came over, and I'm not learning as fast on my own."

Lei and I grew up together, playing in each other's gardens. She's always been like a sister, so it was natural when Daw Widow asked me to teach her to read and write. Spending time with Lei was like being with myself—easy, relaxed, and peaceful. Then, in one instant, everything changed. She was reading a poem by Tin Moe called "Desert Years."

And the earth
like fruit too shy to emerge

without fruit
in shame and sorrow
glances at me
When will the tears change
and the bells ring sweet?

She looked up, and suddenly I couldn't breathe. Had her dark brown eyes always glowed like smooth, polished stones? When did her lips get as red as the flame tree that flowered between our houses? I got to my feet quickly. "Lesson's over," I mumbled.

But too many times since then, I've reread the poem to myself, picturing Lei's smile and smooth skin. And now something deep inside starts trembling whenever she's near. I've even stopped going over there in the afternoons, afraid that Lei will notice how my feelings have changed. Or even worse—that her mother might.

Even now Daw Widow is studying me closely. "You grow more like a bamboo pole by the day," she says. "Taller and skinnier. *And* you need a haircut."

Mother comes out carrying a tray. Tea's still cheap, and this morning she splurged on a small packet of biscuits from the vendor who comes to the door. The biscuits are arranged in a neat fan on the one porcelain plate we haven't sold.

"I'll give you some recipes, Wei-Lin," Daw Widow continues. "My tamarind shrimp soup will fatten this boy up in no time. Teach? Hah! He can barely stand on his own two feet!"

Mother's dimple creases her cheek as she catches my eye. "Does my boy look too thin to you, Lei, dear?" she asks, pouring another cup of tea.

Lei smiles shyly. "No, Daw Wei-Lin. Chiko looks just as ha—I mean, just as healthy as ever."

Healthy? I think. What was she about to say? I push my glasses back up my nose. Stupid things, always falling forward at the wrong time.

"Tell us more about your plan, Chiko," Daw Widow says suddenly.

"They're giving a teaching exam this afternoon at city hall," I say, handing her the newspaper. "Ignorance is bad for Burma, the government says. This time they might be telling the truth. I could pass the exam if Mother lets me go."

Daw Widow's eyes narrow as she studies my face. "So! Somebody who can read a book or use a pencil is smarter than somebody who can't?"

Too late I remember that Daw Widow never learned to read or write. "I didn't mean that," I say, taking the newspaper back. "It's just that I want to do something worthwhile. Make a difference, like Father."

"Humph," Daw Widow snorts. She's quiet for a bit, thinking something over. Then, "Let him go, Wei-Lin."

4

I can't believe my ears. Daw Widow is usually just as bad as Mother when it comes to me leaving the house. The only place I go without the two of them stopping me is next door to teach Lei. I feel a twinge of shame as I recognize the truth. Deep inside I was counting on Daw Widow to keep me from going, to convince Mother it's safer for me to stay inside. Then I could tell myself at least I *tried* to keep my promise.

"What, Ah-Ma?" Mother asks. "You want Chiko to leave me here alone?"

"I'll take care of you," Daw Widow tells her grimly, glaring at the door.

I wish for the hundredth time that Daw Widow had been with us when the soldiers came for Father. Even armed officers would have a hard time standing up to her. I've seen a burly chicken seller back away from her door when she accused him of overcharging her. But she and Lei were visiting relatives the week Father was arrested. Sometimes I wonder if the government was informed of their travel plans.

"I'll keep you company every day, Daw Wei-Lin," Lei adds.

I glance at her face, hoping for any hint of sorrow or worry on my behalf. But how could any girl admire a boy like me? Lei deserves a real man, a hero, a warrior who can protect her. Not a boy hiding inside his mother's house.

Daw Widow takes a sip of tea. "He may act like a good-for-nothing, Wei-Lin, but your boy can teach. I've seen my own girl reading and writing like a scholar these days, thanks to him."

"I know he's smart," Mother says. "And teaching is a noble job. As fine as healing. But how do we know they're not lying? It's not safe for him out there."

"It's not safe in this house either, Nyi-Ma," Daw Widow says softly.

The tone of her voice makes us stare. What does she mean, it isn't safe for me in this house? I notice she's used a special name for Mother: "Nyi-Ma" means "younger sister," the name used for a close relative. As an older neighbor, Daw Widow usually calls my mother by name, but now she's added an extra tenderness with the term of endearment.

"Not safe, Ah-Ma?"

Daw Widow looks straight into Mother's eyes. "He hasn't registered with the army, like he's supposed to. It might be best for him to go out and apply for this job, even if it's a fake. I heard it in the market. They're coming after your boy. They want him to fight, or they'll put him in prison, too."

I lean back in my chair, shaken. Fear rises in my throat like a sponge and dries my mouth. Mother buries her face in her hands.

The room is still. Then Daw Widow speaks again: "He's Joon's son. And yours. He will endure whatever comes his way. Let him go, Nyi-Ma."

"Are you sure?" Mother asks, lifting her head. She takes the handkerchief Lei offers, and wipes her eyes.

"I feel it in my spirit," Daw Widow answers. She turns to me. "What time is this teacher's exam, Chiko?"

"Four o'clock." I'm trying to keep my voice steady.

"It's just past three now," Daw Widow says. "Get out of that *longyi*. It's best to wear trousers to an exam."

I duck into the other room, take off the comfortable cotton cloth knotted around my waist, and change into

21

a pair of pants. Daw Widow is right—somehow I'll have to survive whatever is in my future. But how? My heart yearns for the old days, when Father was here to keep us safe and I could lose myself in a familiar story, one that ended happily.

Daw Widow smiles when I return. "We have something for you, Chiko. Lei, give the boy his gift, will you? And to Daw Wei-Lin, also."

Lei reaches into her mother's woven bag and takes out two packages. She hands one to me and one to Mother. We open them at the same time and discover matching miniature photographs of Father mounted on cardboard. He looks young in the picture, but his eyes are as keen and kind as the last time I saw them. An ache of missing him takes my breath away. *Stay alive, Father*, I pray. *Please stay alive*. Mother is gazing at her copy of the photo, and a tear curves along her cheek. I reach over and thumb it away.

"It's his graduation photo," Lei says. "One of our relatives from the village works in the college, and he hunted down the negative. We developed them at a shop in town—Mother trusts the man who makes the pictures."

"How can we thank you?" Mother manages to say. "We have no picture of him at all. This is exactly as he looked when we first met."

Suddenly reality hits me. This is Daw Widow's good-bye present. Rumors of the government's interest in me must have reached her ears some time ago. That's why she ordered two copies instead of one.

"Thank you, Daw," I manage. "Thank you a thousand times."

She takes the photo, tucks it into my pocket, and fastens the button. Knowing my habit of keeping pens, money, and other valuables in the front pockets of my shirts, Mother sews sturdy buttons on them so that nothing can fall out.

"No need for thanks," Daw Widow says, giving the pocket a pat. "You better catch a rickshaw before you miss that exam. Many women would want a son-in-law brave enough to try to be a teacher in these terrible times."

My mouth falls open. Have I heard right? I must have. Daw Widow's raisin eyes are twinkling at me. So I haven't been able to hide my feelings for Lei! But what does Lei think? I push my glasses back up and steal a look. But Lei is leaning over Mother's shoulder, studying Father's picture. The veil of silky hair hides her face.

"What are you waiting for, boy?" Daw Widow asks. "Go! And be careful."

"Hurry back before it gets late, Chiko," Mother says, handing me a jacket. "I'll be waiting. It's dangerous out there for a boy your age, so try not to meet the eyes of strangers."

I slip my feet into my sandals, hardly knowing what I'm doing. I haven't left our home much for four months, and when I do, Mother insists on coming along. Am I really heading out into the city on my own?

23

Lei looks up, finally, smiling her sweet smile. I straighten my shoulders. If I have to go, I'll leave with my head high. I can at least pretend I'm a hero.

Mother hands me a few kyat notes. I don't want to take them, but she insists. "Just in case," she says, kissing me. "Please, Chiko."

Daw Widow opens the front door. The light dazzles my eyes, making the house seem even more like a cave.

Pausing on the threshold, I lift my hand. "See you tonight!"

"A lesson tomorrow, Ko?" It's Lei. She's called me "older brother" ever since we were little. I don't mind—girls use that word for their sweethearts, too.

"A lesson tomorrow, Lei!" I answer, and close the door behind me.

5

The rickshaw speeds through the tree-lined streets. I huddle into the back of it, remembering Mother's advice to avoid eye contact.

Sidewalk vendors are beginning to set up wares for the afternoon. The rickshaw veers to avoid children playing in the streets. These little ones should be in school, but they don't have a choice. Schools have been closed so many times that nobody can learn much.

Thanks to Father, I can teach kids like these; I know I can. My work with Lei made me sure of it. But I don't have any formal record of classes or

25

examinations. Will the officials count that against me? I'll have to speak up, stand up for myself, convince them to test my abilities.

The lobby of city hall feels crowded. Young people mill about, mostly boys. Father used to encourage me to join in the neighborhood soccer and cricket games. I'd obey reluctantly and hurry back to my books as soon as I could. But after these months of Mother insisting I stay inside, I've missed being around boys my age. I count ten, including myself, most wearing *longyi* but a couple in trousers, like me. Four girls are also in the room.

"We've been waiting two hours already," says a short, wiry boy to one of the girls. "It must be a lie. Let's go."

I feel a twinge of alarm. Could he be right?

"Let's wait a bit longer, Ko," says the girl, clinging to his arm.

He must be her brother; they're too young to be sweethearts. She looks like she's only about twelve, and the boy just a year or two older. Her faded sarong is as dirty as his *longyi*, and their street accent grates on my ears. Their cheeks are smeared with *tanaka*, a light-colored paste that common people use to protect their skin from the sun. Why are these ragged, illiterate kids even trying to become teachers? Maybe this is a trick. The wiry boy is pulling his sister to the door. I'm so uneasy now that I follow them.

But it's too late.

Bang! A side door bursts open.

Soldiers pour into the room.

They're shouting and waving rifles. I shield my head with my arms. *It was a lie!* I think, my mind racing.

Girls and boys alike are screaming. The soldiers prod and herd some of us together and push the rest apart as if we're cows or goats. Their leader is a middle-aged man. He's moving slowly, intently, not dashing around like the others.

"Take the boys only, Win Min," I overhear him telling a tall, gangly soldier. "Make them obey."

"Yes, Father," the soldier answers immediately, jabbing the butt of his rifle into the boy wearing the torn shirt.

The boy cries out and collapses. Was he hit *that* hard? Is he all right?

Cursing and shoving soldiers surround him and me and the rest of the boys. One of them shouts at the other side of the room, "You—girls! Go home. *Now!*"

Three of the girls obey quickly, escaping through the door, braids flying behind them. Only the girl in the faded sarong stays, her eyes fixed on the boy beside me. He's still hunched over, one hand on his back where the rifle hit him.

The tall soldier, Win Min, strides over. "Go!" he tells the girl.

"No! My brother and I came together!" The girl's voice is hard. "They're supposed to be hiring street sweepers, the radio said."

Street sweepers? I *have* come to the wrong place. I'll tell them there's been a mistake.

"Go home, girl. Tell your family your brother has a job. He'll send money. Now leave. *Quickly!*"

"No!"

Swearing, the soldier grabs the girl and tries to drag her to the door.

She flails her fists in his face, twisting and squirming to loosen his grip. "I'm not leaving without him!" she screams. The soldier raises the stock of his rifle.

The boy straightens up suddenly. "Go!"

His sister stops fighting and is shoved outside, but I can still hear her wailing. The soldiers begin to steer the boys toward the door.

I manage to catch the captain's sleeve. "Sir," I say. "I came to take a teaching exam. There's been a mistake—"

I catch his sideways glance as he yanks his sleeve out of my hand and steps back.

And then I can hardly believe what happens next. The tall soldier is there before I know it. He sways back on one foot. He lifts his other high in the air and smashes his boot against my jaw. Hard.

I fall on the tiled floor, gasping for air. The whole side of my head is on fire.

"Get up," the soldier tells me. "Our captain doesn't make mistakes."

Most boys learn to take and give blows when they're

young, but this is the first time I've been struck, and I'm shaking with shock and pain. I manage to get up somehow and join the rest of the boys, clutching my jaw and straightening my glasses, which fell askew with the kick.

A battered army bus waits in the street. Rickshaw drivers perch on their cycles, arms folded, pretending not to watch. It's no use calling for help—people hurry past, eyes down, wanting to avoid trouble. Can I make a run for it, taking cover behind the rickshaws? At least get a message to one of the drivers for Daw Widow?

But the soldiers flank our line. The street boy is behind me. His sister, hurling insults and threats, tries to fight her way to him, but she's pushed back roughly. When it's my turn, there's nothing to do but climb aboard, my heart racing, my sweaty shirt clinging to my back.

I find a seat by a window. My chin and cheek are starting to swell. The short, wiry boy in the torn shirt slides in beside me. His hair is spiky and sticks up like a bush. With the *tanaka* paste smeared on his cheeks, he reminds me of an act in the circus that used to come to Yangon.

Taking the front rows and lighting cigarettes, the young soldiers boast loudly about how easy it was to gather us up. The captain chooses a seat in the middle of the bus, just behind the tall soldier, two rows ahead of me. The bus starts moving. Pushing me back, the street boy leans across my chest and thrusts his head though the open window. His sister is sprinting beside the bus.

"Let him go!" she shouts. The bus picks up speed, and the girl can no longer keep up. "Ko!" I can hear the desperation in her last cry.

"Stay near the tea shop!" the boy shouts. "I'll come back for you!"

At least he got to say good-bye.

The captain's head swivels, and his eyes glitter under the bushy single line of his eyebrows. Cigarette clenched between his teeth, he watches my half-standing seatmate. The street boy, to my amazement, stares right back. For a long minute, their eyes meet. Then the captain takes a drag on his cigarette. Smoke puffs out of his mouth and wafts toward us.

I'm reminded of a picture in *The Arabian Nights* of a genie casting a spell on a captive prince. The captain's magic works just as well. The boy beside me sits down and closes his eyes, lids dropping like window blinds.

6

I try to soothe my bruised face against the cold glass as the bus hurtles along. Is this really happening? Where are they taking us? When will they bring us back? I have to keep track of the journey so that I can send word home about my location.

We're already on the outskirts of the city and heading north, where rice paddies and coconut trees line the narrow, flat highway. Women are harvesting rice, their bodies bent, their bamboo hats shaped like upside-down bowls. Thin, straight streams sparkle like wires, dividing the

31

wet fields into squares. The last rays of the sun redden, spilling into the water like blood.

How will Mother feel when I don't come back? Will she be able to sleep alone in the house? I remind myself of Daw Widow; she'll never leave Mother alone. I think of Lei and rub my eyes, thankful that my seatmate's are still closed.

The last light disappears behind the coconut trees. *Coward, Chiko!* I tell myself. *Be a man!* I try to picture Father, remembering how steady his voice was as he called out that last request even as the soldiers were pulling him away. If only I could hear that calm voice again! Or catch one more glimpse of his face! I need to know he's somewhere on the planet, breathing, talking, healing, trying his best to get home.

Suddenly I remember the gift Lei and her mother gave me. I unbutton my pocket and fumble inside. Is Father's photo gone? Did it fall out in the confusion? No, thanks to Mother's strong sewing, everything in my pocket is safe, including the money she gave me. I'm about to take Father's photo out when I notice the captain is still half-turned in his seat. I can't risk losing this gift, and I don't want another kick; I'll have to wait until later. Quickly I refasten the pocket button and zip up my jacket.

A few of the soldiers start singing a popular song from a film. One looks like he's only about fourteen. *Village boys,* I think, listening to their accents. The captain takes off his military jacket, leans forward, and tells a joke. His soldiers laugh as though it's the funniest thing they've heard. That joke is stale in the city; I've heard vendors who come to our door tell it a dozen times.

Win Min turns and folds his commanding officer's jacket carefully. The captain pats the gangly boy's shoulder, making him beam.

The bus rattles on as it grows dark, but I manage to keep track of our direction, thanks to Father's geography lessons. Now we're heading northeast toward Thailand. We'll soon reach the hilly country, where tribal people plant rice. Father used to tell me about people like the Shan, the Wa, and the Kayah, who call themselves the Karenni. The government is trying to get rid of them and take their land, but they have a right to be a part of our country. After all, they've lived here for centuries.

The bus begins to swerve as the road curves uphill. A chilly breeze blows through the top half of the window, and I struggle to close it. The street boy sits up and reaches to help. Our eyes meet briefly. He looks even younger now than when I first spotted him. How old is he, anyway?

"My sons," the captain says suddenly in a loud voice. "Tell these new recruits our policy about escaping from camp."

"I will, Father," Win Min answers, jumping to his feet

and lowering his head. Why does he call that man his father? "You won't try to escape, believe me. You'll be guarded until your training is finished, in case one of you is stupid enough to try. The six of us are the captain's best men in this platoon. He counts on us like sons. A few of you could rise through the ranks and join us. If you're brave enough, that is."

The boy beside me grunts. "We're going to a military camp," he mutters. "Ready to be a soldier?"

A soldier? Me? No! I can't fight! I have to get off this bus! But we're already miles from the city, climbing higher into the mountains along the border. I swallow hard and rest my head against the glass.

A voice whispers near my ear: "We'll escape. I'll find a way."

If I weren't so anxious, I'd laugh. Escape? With soldiers everywhere, assigned to watch us day and night? Is this boy really that stupid? I turn away and close my eyes.

7

After what seems like endless hours through the dark mountains, the bus stops with a jolt. The driver turns off the engine. The captain and his soldiers climb down first.

"Recruits out!" someone shouts.

One by one we emerge into the cool night air. The captain watches us disembark, and a shiver runs through me as I feel his keen gaze. I pull my jacket tightly around me and follow the others. The street boy stays close to me.

It's hard to see anything in the dark. All I can make out is one wide, low building, another smaller one, and a muddy, open field between them. We enter the larger building, with the soldiers filing in after us and the captain bringing up the rear. About two dozen other soldiers are milling about inside, but they stiffen into attention as soon as the captain enters.

This place was once a gym, and two netless rims stand like sentries at either end of the hall. A few kerosene lamps spill pools of yellow light onto the hard floor, and blankets are piled here and there. A large poster is taped over the entrance. Military Training Centre, it declares.

A short, squat man walks over. Like the captain, this man is older, and the younger soldiers lower their heads before they salute him. In turn, he bows and salutes to the captain. "I am Sergeant U-Tha-Din," he tells us. "I am in charge of this platoon's training. We specialize in jungle warfare and search-and-destroy operations against insurgents and narcotics-based armies. Two sections have already almost completed their training, and you're next. Any questions?"

"I'm hungry," somebody behind me calls. "When do we eat?"

"Tomorrow," answers the sergeant, receiving a loud groan in response.

One of the soldiers who captured us speaks up. "You spoiled city brats don't know the meaning of the word *hungry*. But you'll find out. Right, Father?"

Their "father" is standing in a corner. The word still

sounds strange, but so many boys my age have lost their real fathers. Maybe they're looking for a replacement.

The captain nods, his eyes searching the room. They find the wiry boy beside me and then move over to measure me. I feel pinned under his cold stare; a wave of nausea rises through my stomach. Why is he focusing on us?

The street boy yawns. I can hardly believe it. Here I am, trying to keep from throwing up, and this kid is about to take a nap. Doesn't he realize the man has singled him out?

"We'll fit you for your uniforms in the morning, but for now you each get one blanket and a *longyi* to wear at night," the sergeant says, pointing to two piles on the floor. "You'll store your belongings beneath your blankets during the day—there is no stealing in this camp. Why? Because *everyone* joins in when we beat a thief." He holds up a battered tin cup. "There's one of these for each of you, too. Get water from the river across the field. It's well past midnight already, so make it quick, and don't use the river for a toilet. Go into the trees behind the field for that, at least for now. Part of your training will include building latrines for the camp. The bell will ring at five thirty."

Three soldiers with flashlights and rifles lead us to the river. The rest of them disappear into the smaller building. I lose sight of the captain, which worries me. My instincts warn me to keep him in sight.

As I dip my cup into the shallows, I think of the times

I complained about pumping water from the well in our garden. If only I could be there right now, with Mother waiting inside the house. If only this were all a bad dream.

The bus that brought us here starts up, and I listen until the sound of it disappears. Around us the jungle looms, dark and dangerous. I stumble back across the field into the gym after the other boys, who scramble for the blankets and *longyi*. There aren't any left by the time I get there.

8

The *tanaka* boy has managed to grab an extra blanket and *longyi*. He tosses them to me, and I take them reluctantly. Is this tough-talking kid going to stick to me like the paste on his cheeks? It'll be easier to stay safe if I keep to myself. *One day at a time, Chiko. That's how you're going to survive this. Mind your own business. And stay out of trouble.*

Somebody locks us in from the outside, and three soldiers, all "sons" of the captain, stand guard by the doors. I find an empty spot along one wall, and the street boy arranges his blanket right next to mine. I turn and study the wall. A small plaque is attached to it. The words are inscribed in an unfamiliar script. They look like some kind of tribal language, but there are English words below them that I can read: Karenni Bible College Gymnasium, Dedicated to God, January 1984.

So this once belonged to the tribal people. What happened to them? How did the Burmese army get the gym?

"I'm getting out of here," my neighbor whispers. "Want to come with me?"

"We're locked in," I mutter, keeping my back to him. Not to mention that soldiers are leaning against the door, rifles propped beside them.

He grunts. "I mean tomorrow morning. They won't lock us in during the day. Doesn't seem like there's a fence around the camp."

I can't keep the irritation out of my voice. "They don't need one. This place is surrounded by jungle. We're miles from anywhere. Besides, he'll have other ways to keep us in—" I can't finish. Fear coils in my stomach at the thought of the captain's sinister glare.

"I'll find a way out. I *have* to get to my sister."

The urgency in his voice is so intense I turn to face him. The outline of his body seems small in the dim light of the gym. "*You're* in more trouble than your sister," I tell him. "She's probably safe at home by now."

A shudder goes through the boy's body. "I have to get out of here," he says again. "I have to get to her."

"She'll tell your parents what happened."

The boy is quiet. Then he says, "We have no parents. It's just the two of us. On the streets."

I can't think of anything to say. Yangon is full of orphans who work or scavenge for food by day and sleep on the streets at night. They roam in pairs as protection against robbers and kidnappers. What will his sister do now that she's alone?

"What's your name?" the boy asks, breaking the silence.

"Chiko."

"How old are you?"

"Fifteen."

"So am I!" he says.

I can't believe we're the same age—he looks so much younger.

"I'm Tai," he says.

We're quiet again. Mother used to give food to street kids who came to our door. She might even have fed these two.

"Your sister—she didn't seem scared," I say. "She called those soldiers some interesting names."

Tai snorts. "She's crazy. Not much I can do to stop her when she gets angry."

"She's smart, too." I add.

"You're right. She's always been smarter than me, anyway. Well, worrying all night won't help anything. I'll

41

need a good night's sleep if I'm going to escape. See you in the morning, Chiko."

Before I can answer, he pulls the blanket over his head. In a minute or two I hear steady, even breaths beside me. A street boy can fall asleep anywhere, I suppose. The floor is hard, the air damp, and the blanket doesn't cover my whole body. I shift around, trying not to think of my own bed at home.

After Father was arrested I used to have nightmares. As soon as she heard me shout, Mother would come rushing to my room. How I wish I could feel her cool palm on my forehead and hear her soft voice singing me back to sleep! What am I doing in this godforsaken place? How will I survive the "training" that starts tomorrow?

Shifting again, I feel something dig into my chest. It's Father's photo; I'd forgotten all about it. I prop myself on an elbow, keeping a wary eye on the guards. There's just enough light from the one kerosene lamp still flickering nearby. But as I reach inside my pocket, my fingers find two small squares of cardboard, not one. Suddenly I remember how Daw Widow patted my pocket just before I left. She must have added something else. What in the world could it be?

I study both gifts in the dim light. One is the photograph of Father, of course. The other, to my amazement, is a black-and-white version of Lei, staring solemnly out at me. I can't believe it! Daw Widow must know how I feel! And she doesn't mind—in fact, this surprise is like getting her blessing. And wait—Lei must have known about the gift, too. Didn't she say they went together to pick up the photos?

I gaze at Lei's picture for a long time, my heart racing. Her face is still and serious in the pose, but it's easy for my imagination to add the sparkle in her eyes, the shimmer to her clothes, that sweet, light scent of jasmine, her teasing smile. Desire for the flesh-and-blood Lei slices through me like a sword. Now that I know how she feels, I won't be so shy when I get back. If I get back.

I study Father's photo again. There he is, a few years older than I am now, gazing steadily into an unknown future. *Try hard, my son,* he used to say before our study sessions. *That's all I ask.*

I put the photos back into my pocket. The light flickers and goes out, and the gym is dark. Taking off my glasses, I cradle the puffy side of my face in one palm and try to fall asleep.

9

Someone yanks the blanket off my body.

I jump up, startled. *Where am I? Where's Mother?*

My heart sinks as I recognize the soldiers who brought us here. So yesterday wasn't a nightmare. I fumble for my glasses, change into my trousers, and put on my jacket.

They lead us out to the field, into a misty, gray dawn. Shivering in my thin clothes, I notice Tai beside me. He's wearing only a *longyi* and a torn T-shirt, but he doesn't even look cold. Instead, he pats his belly and tips his head in the direction of a tarp, under which a few soldiers cluster around a cooking fire. My own stomach rumbles in reply; the last meal I ate was lunch yesterday, with Mother.

I look around while we wait for the food. We're in a valley shaped like a flat-bottomed bowl, with dense, green slopes curving up on every side. Roosters crow in the distance. The river where we filled our cups the night before cuts the valley in half. Beyond it are paddies and a farmhouse nestled at the foot of high hills. Jungle covers the hills behind us, swallowing the dirt road that leads back up the mountain.

The sections of trained soldiers eat first, under the tarp. Soon, though, they come to the field and hand us cups of weak tea and bowls of steaming rice. I devour my food, but I'm not as fast as Tai. He's licking the bowl clean with his tongue before I'm halfway done. I glance at my bowl once I'm full; there's still some rice stuck to the sides. I've probably got a lot more stored inside me than this street boy. I hand my bowl to him, and he flashes me a grin of gratitude before licking mine clean, too.

After breakfast we're fitted for uniforms. The jacket and trousers are made of faded green cloth and look ancient, with buttons missing and patches here and there. Mine smell like somebody died in them, but I put them on. They're warm, at least. They don't give us shirts, so we have to wear our own. And there aren't enough boots to go around, so half of us don't get any. Of course, I'm one of the new recruits who stays in sandals.

We hear an engine in the distance. I tell myself I'm crazy to hope, but maybe they realized they made a mistake. Maybe the bus is coming to take some of us back. Instead a jeep screeches to a stop, and the captain gets out. The sight of his angular face makes the hair prickle on the back of my neck. Where has he been all night? Why didn't he stay in the barracks with the others? And I don't like the look of that bamboo stick he's carrying—the end is sharpened like the tip of a spear.

The soldiers prod us into a 3–3–4 formation, almost a square. It seems to me that I'm one of the older boys in this section. A couple of them can't be more than twelve. We look different now that we're in uniform, more like one unit, despite the variances in height and weight.

After returning salutes from the sergeant and the other soldiers, the captain approaches us with a smile, swinging his stick with each step. He's flanked quickly by six of the soldiers who captured us in the city.

"You were hoping to serve your country, boys," he tells us, his voice smooth and kind. "Well, you've been accepted. Each of you will receive monthly pay for your service, money that will either be sent back to your family in Yangon or given to you here."

My heart skips a beat. If only what he's saying is true! If we do get monthly pay, I'll be able to take care of Mother, just as Father asked.

"I hope they pay us soon," Tai mutters. "I'd like to take the money with me."

The captain turns to Tai. "You said something?" His voice is low and controlled, but a muscle in his cheek twitches.

Tai lifts his chin. "I was wondering when we'd be paid, sir."

The captain's mouth keeps smiling, but his eyes are steely. "That's a reasonable question. You'll be paid *after* one month of service. Your term of service is three years unless you're wounded in battle."

Three years? How will I survive three years? I try to focus on the fact that we're actually going to be paid. Mother will be able to give the landlord the rent we owe for the past few months and buy meat, fish, eggs, and milk. She'll be able to send more for Father's upkeep, too. And all I have to do is survive. *Stay alive. Keep out of trouble. One day at a time.* The words could become a chant, like the ones the Buddhist monks use to ward off evil. *Mind your own business. Keep out of trouble. Stay alive. One day at a time.*

The captain is pacing around our square of ten recruits. "Beloved sons of Burma," he says. His voice is rich and deep, the timbre reminding me almost of Father's. "Why does your country need you to fight on her behalf?"

Good question, I think, but I don't let it show on my face.

47

"You could be home, safe and sound, studying, working, teaching"—here he pauses and looks directly at me—"were it not for the tribal people. They want to break our country apart and divide it among themselves. Their whole mission is to destroy our peace. If we succeed in defeating these insurgents, we can return home to care for our mothers and sisters." He flicks Tai a glance before continuing.

"You may have heard that the rebels who call themselves the Kayah are among the most evil of our enemies." *They call themselves the Karenni, actually. Father used to tell me about a good Karenni friend he had in school.*

I've been taught not to believe anything the government says about the tribal people. But the other new recruits didn't have someone to tell them the truth. All they have is this captain's version.

He's still talking and pacing, smiling, his voice calm and kind. "Many have turned away from the teachings of the Buddha to embrace Western religions, in the hope that they can gain weapons from America to attack us. They are ruthless killers, men and women alike, and they despise our Burmese language and our Buddhist religion."

He tells us about a pair of elderly women who were killed by rebel warriors. "They were minding their own business, like grandmothers do, sewing and chatting in the shade of a mango grove, when a pack of rebels stormed out of the jungle and . . ."

Except for Tai and me, the other boys are nodding, listening, spellbound. I should stand and challenge his version of the truth; I should tell them not to trust him so easily. But I stay where I am, slouched and low. Next to me, Tai yawns.

The captain notices. He and his soldiers are quite close to us now, so I catch the quick look he gives his "son" Win Min. Then he lowers his head ever so slightly and leaves his bamboo stick at Tai's feet.

Immediately Win Min goes into action. "What happens if you don't complete your three years?" he asks in a loud voice, his face inches from Tai's.

"I'll be punished?" answers Tai.

"You'll be *severely* punished," Win Min says. "Do you understand?"

Tai shrugs. "Yes."

Win Min glances at the captain before picking up the stick. "Say that like you mean it, boy," he says, whacking the bamboo across Tai's legs.

But Tai is ready for the blow. Just before the stick makes contact, he leaps back and cries out as if he's in agony. The stick lands lightly, thanks to Tai's move. Glowering, Win Min raises his weapon again and steps forward.

"That's enough, my son," the captain says, reaching for the stick. "Nobody is going to try to shirk this duty. Why would they want to? It is an honorable service, we take

49

good care of you here, you have plenty to eat, and we'll be sending money to your families."

I take a quick look at Tai's shins. No sign of blood. As Win Min steps back, blocking the captain's line of vision, Tai winks at me. My heart lifts. That street boy's so good at deception, it's scary. I'm glad he's not hurt.

10

A truck roars down the hill, coming to a stop behind the captain's jeep. The bed is full of cinder blocks, lime, and other building materials I don't recognize.

The captain turns to the sergeant. "These recruits should spend the rest of the morning working on the latrines. Begin defense training in the afternoon. I'll return tomorrow."

"Yes, sir," Sergeant U-Tha-Din answers. "I'll make sure they give their full effort for Mother Burma."

The sergeant assigns Tai, two others, and me the

task of hauling blocks from the truck to the construction site, and the rest of the recruits start digging. I groan as I calculate how many trips we'll need to unload the whole truck. After months at home doing nothing but reading and writing, my arms and legs are reed thin and weak.

The other two boys join me, each of us carrying one bulky block at a time, but Tai is nowhere in sight. Where is he? Has he found a way to sneak off and avoid the work? I trudge back and forth, concentrating on the slowly growing pile. My glasses keep slipping down my nose, and I take them off and tuck them into my pocket. After a few more trips, I stop in surprise. How has the pile of blocks grown so quickly?

I squint and spot Tai trotting back to the site from the far side of the truck. He's balancing a bamboo pole across his bony shoulders. On either end of the pole, he's tied slings out of cloth he's found somewhere. He's hauling four blocks at a time, two on either end of the pole. And he isn't sweating like the rest of us.

He grins at me. "Make one for yourself," he says, jerking his head toward the truck.

A few loose bamboo poles are scattered on the ground, and some rags are piled on the bed of the truck. As I try to make a contraption like Tai's, he comes over to help. His fingers are nimble, and he ties intricate knots in the rags—knots I've never seen before. I test them by pulling as hard as I can, and they hold fast.

The other boys come to see what we're doing. Soon all four of us are using Tai's sling method of lugging blocks. The truck is empty before the sun has climbed too high in the sky. U-Tha-Din's broad face creases into a wide smile as he inspects our work. "Take a rest, boys," he says. "You've worked hard."

I stretch my tired legs in front of me. Tai is flat on his back, spiky hair even more untidy than before, the last traces of the *tanaka* paste on his face making him look like he has a disease. Mother always told me not to judge people by their appearance. She was certainly right in Tai's case.

11

We need that brief break. The rest of the day is even more grueling than hauling rocks. The afternoon defense training means running around the field in endless circles, climbing trees, and kickboxing soldiers eager to show how strong they got during *their* training.

Tai encourages me as I run, keeping pace beside me. He teaches me to find footholds on the trees, and he stays underneath me as though he knows I'm scared to fall. He even kickboxes two soldiers instead of one without anybody guessing I've missed my turn. Both times he's flat on the ground within moments. His groans and shouts of pain make my stomach turn, but he jumps to his feet quickly as the next boys begin to battle.

That night, after bathing in the river and changing into *longyi*, the two of us take our spots on the floor of the gym, leaning wearily against the wall. Every muscle in my body aches. I glance at Tai's face. His eyes are closed, but I can tell he's awake. Other boys are talking quietly throughout the gym. The guards don't seem to mind as long as we keep our voices low.

"Those soldiers seem to enjoy being rough," I whisper. "Especially that Win Min. Can't they remember their own training and have some mercy?"

Tai snorts without opening his eyes. "You call that rough? Try living for a week on the streets."

He's right. I don't know anything about surviving the streets of Yangon. I'd probably be dead after a day.

"My father's in prison." I want him to know my life hasn't been easy just because I have parents and a home.

"For what?"

"Accused of being a traitor to the nation."

"Have you heard from him?"

I take a deep breath. "No. It's been four months."

"What's he like?"

The memory of Father calling my name echoes in my mind. "He was—I mean is," I correct myself quickly, "a brave man. The best doctor in Yangon."

I hate that my voice is shaky, but Tai doesn't comment.

"U-Tha-Din seems okay," he says after a while. "Dumb, but not mean."

"Unlike that captain," I say.

"The one-eyebrowed idiot? Don't worry, I can handle Captain Evil."

"He's trouble," I say. "Stay away from him, Tai."

"Don't worry about me. I've known men like that all my life."

"He's lying about the war. About the tribal people."

"I'm not sure about that," Tai says. "War is war. Terrible things happen."

I put my hand over my pocket. Will Mother and Lei be safe in Yangon? At least Daw Widow is there to protect them.

"Tomorrow I'm going to escape," Tai says. "Want to join me?"

"Are you crazy?" I ask. "You heard what they said. I have to stay alive. I promised Father I'd take care of Mother."

"You'll never survive here. You're a teacher, not a soldier. Look at that inky bump on your finger. That's the biggest muscle in your whole body."

He's right, but I can't help resenting his description. My irritation must have shown because Tai smiles. "I don't mean to make you feel bad, Chiko," he says. "I can't read and write, so I'd never make it in school. But if I were going to stay in this place, I could survive. I'm just not sure you'll be able to."

56

I remember how quickly he got up after being kicked down by two soldiers. "You're right," I admit, swallowing my pride. "I'm not in the best physical condition. All study and no work hasn't been good for me. How do you handle such hard hits without getting injured?"

"I can teach you," he says. "I've taken plenty of kicks and punches."

"That sounds good. Tell you what—if you teach me how to survive this training, I'll teach you to read and write."

He's quiet for a while. Then he speaks as if thinking out loud. "If I weren't leaving, I'd accept your offer. I can do math, but reading and writing might get me a job in a store or something better."

I don't want to remind him of his sister's plight but decide to take the risk. "She'll be okay for a while without you," I say.

"She can't stay at the temple tea shop forever. . . . No, I have to get out of here, Chiko."

The memory of Mother's face dances in front of my eyes. Maybe I can help. "I have an idea, Tai."

He shrugs. "Don't waste it on my account. I'll be in Yangon by tomorrow night."

I get up and walk to one of the soldiers guarding the door. "Do you have paper and a pencil?"

The chubby soldier is big but young, and his thick accent marks him as a villager. "What?" he asks, blinking at me in the dim light.

"Hey, Bindu!" another guard calls across the room. "That four-eyes giving you trouble?"

"Uhh . . . no," the soldier answers. He draws closer. "You can write?" he whispers, his eyes wide.

I nod.

"There might be some old supplies in that box over there," the soldier says, still keeping his voice low.

I nod my thanks and rummage through the odds and ends. I find one piece of yellowed paper and a stub of a pencil and take them back to my place against the wall. Tai's almost asleep; he yawns when I tell him I'm writing a letter to my mother.

"What's your sister's name?" I ask. "And where's the temple?"

"Sawati," he says sleepily. "And it's the big temple in the center of town. Now be quiet and go to sleep. I have to save my strength for tomorrow."

Dear Mother, I write. *I have been recruited to join the army. But please don't worry. They are feeding us well, and my body will become stronger. You will receive my paycheck every month, enough kyats each time to cover the rent and a bit more. Stay safe and I will return to you soon. Give my greetings to Daw Widow.*

I pause and then keep writing.

Thank her for the presents she gave me. They will sustain me through the long days and nights. Mother, will you do one thing for me? Go with Daw Widow to the tea shop at the big temple and ask for a girl named Sawati. She's a good girl and will be a help to you. Her brother is here, and he's very worried about her. I know you will care for her. Send an answer back with this driver once you have found her. I love you, dear Mother. Your son, Chiko.

I fold the letter and put Mother's address on it. Glancing around, I take a kyat note from my pocket and tuck it into the letter. The driver might need some convincing to deliver it.

12

The next morning Tai's body is a silent lump under his blanket. I put on my uniform and creep out of the gym. The soldiers who kept guard overnight are cooking and getting ready for the day's work. The field is covered with mist, so they don't notice me heading for the truck.

The driver grunts when I slip him the letter along with the kyat note. He holds the bill up against the sky where the sun is about to rise. Then he tucks both the letter and the money into his pocket.

I hurry to where the other recruits are gathering to eat. The mist is lifting, and the edge of the sky is the color of a ripe mango. Soon the valley sparkles with the first rays of the sun. I'm hoping the truck will leave soon; the driver is finishing his breakfast. Just as he turns on the engine, though, a jeep drives up, blocking the truck's exit. My heart sinks as the captain gets out. He's alone, driving himself this time.

"Recruits fall in!" U-Tha-Din orders.

Quickly we line up. Three straight rows of three boys each. Beside me in the last row, Tai's spot is empty. Where is he? Suddenly I remember his wild plan of escape.

The captain strides over. "Where's your friend, Teacher?" he asks me. The word is tinged with sarcasm, and I wonder if the other boys notice it.

"I don't know, s-s-sir," I stammer. My hands begin shaking, and I clasp them together to make them stop. Now it looks like I'm praying. Maybe I am. I can still feel the thud of the tall soldier's kick landing on my jawbone. Will I be hit again?

But the captain turns to the sergeant instead. "Another example of your poor leadership, U-Tha-Din," he says. "Come with me, Teacher."

He leads me across the field and behind the barracks, where the others can't see us. Pulling off my glasses with his free hand, he swings them with two fingers in front of my face. "I never want to see you wearing these again," he says, and drops them.

I lunge to try and catch them, but it's too late. I hear

a crunch under his feet. Those glasses cost my parents a lot of money. Now I can't focus on things that are close; I won't be able to read or write.

The man can see into my mind. "You won't need to read here," he says, keeping his voice low. "Time to wake up, Teacher."

His hand moves so fast I don't see it coming. Slamming against the same side of my face that Win Min bruised two days before, the captain's hand lands even harder than the soldier's foot. My head snaps to the side; my entire skull shudders with pain.

"The street boy," he says in a low voice near my ear. "Where is he?"

I put my hands up to shield my face. "I don't know."

"Crying?" he asks. "Never learned to be a man at school, did you? Where is he?"

"I . . . I don't know."

Smack! My head snaps the other way. I'm dizzy now and feel like I might faint.

"Stupid boy," he says. "Stand up straight. Let's go."

He leads me to Win Min. I brace myself for another blow, but the tall soldier doesn't kick me. Not yet, anyway. Instead he cups his hands around his mouth. "Tell us where the street boy is, Teacher, or I'll kick your head in!" he bellows across the field.

"Don't hurt him!" It's Tai. He's climbing out from under the canvas piled in the back of the truck bed.

Win Min gallops toward Tai, stick uplifted. Soldiers and recruits push forward in their eagerness to watch.

I seize my chance, darting behind the barracks and fumbling in the tall grass for my glasses. Good—here they are! The left lens is cracked, but the lens for the right eye is okay. At least I'll be able to see through one eye. I put the glasses into my pocket and dash back, hoping nobody noticed.

Nobody did. They're all focused on Tai and the soldier. My glasses are for reading, so even without them I can see what's happening at a distance. Tai is on the ground at Win Min's feet. He's trying to scramble to his feet, but before he can stand, the soldier kicks him in the ribs. Tai shouts in pain, and his body writhes on the ground.

The captain, like me, is standing behind most of the soldiers and recruits. He swivels his head and looks at me. I sense that he's waiting for me to do something, and I try to move out of his line of vision. *One day at a time. Mind your own business. Stay out of trouble.*

Win Min kicks Tai again.

Tai shrieks, twisting and squirming. He tries to roll away, but it's no use. His body seems smaller than ever as he curls into a ball.

Win Min raises his voice so we can hear him over Tai's shouts and wails. "This is what happens if you try to escape."

His boot pounds against Tai's body again and again.

I want to run forward to stop him, but I don't. Instead I stuff my fingers in my ears to block out the screaming.

Finally it stops. I let my hands drop, and push forward through the onlookers. Tai is crumpled and still. For a moment I think he's dead, but a low groan comes from his body.

"Get up, street scum," Win Min says.

The captain moves to stand beside me. "Enough for that one, Win Min," he says quietly. "What happens if you try to help someone escape?"

I turn to run, but it's too late. The tall soldier blocks me, sneering. "Let's not forget the teacher, who tried to cover up for the street rat."

Thwack! His boot slams into my chest—not as hard as the captain's private beating, but still hard enough to send me sprawling across the dirt.

13

The other recruits back away. I'm flat on the ground, just a few meters or so from Tai. I stay there until the captain stalks off to the barracks, followed first by his loyal cadre and then by the other trained soldiers. That's when I crawl to where Tai is stirring.

"Tai? Are you—? Can you—?" I whisper.

"I'm not bad," Tai gasps, wincing as he feels his ribs. "Nothing's broken. What about you?"

"I'm okay," I say, even though it's still hard to breathe. I glance around. The sergeant is headed for the river, and the other recruits are following him. Slowly I get up and offer my hand to Tai.

"Thanks." Tai lets me haul him to his feet.

I don't meet his eye. *For what?* I want to ask. *For standing there while that thug almost killed you?*

"What were you saying to the driver?" he whispers. "You did a great job of distracting him. For a second I thought you didn't see me climbing into the back."

I didn't. I focus on his first question. "Weren't you listening last night? I sent a letter to Mother asking her to take care of your sister. The driver will bring an answer when he returns."

"You did that? For me?" Tai tries to smile, but he's still clutching his side and his breath is ragged. "I won't forget that, Chiko. Where are your glasses?"

"I've got them. He crushed one lens, but I can still see out of the other. He told me not to wear them, though."

Tai reaches out and clasps my hand as we head to the river, where the other recruits are gathering. It's a strange sensation. This is how men walk with a good friend, a best friend: hand in hand. A first for me.

When we reach the boys in our section, a few murmur greetings and ask if we're okay.

"I'm fine," Tai assures them.

I'm not, I want to say. My skull feels like it's shattered, and my ribs are bruised. But Tai's beating was much worse than mine. "I'm all right."

U-Tha-Din begins to describe our task for the day. "We have to gather stones from the middle of the river and bring them to the construction site. The farmer across the river wants us to arrange the rest of the stones so the current runs into his irrigation channels with more force. In return, he is going to provide us with eggs and milk every day."

The whole section cheers. Eggs and milk are a luxury, even in the city. Everybody starts working hard. As we lift stones from the river and lug them across the field, I keep an eye on Tai to see if he needs help. But he's made of tougher fiber than I am. By the afternoon he's outrunning me again, carrying big rocks, gaining energy by the minute. His sandaled feet are bleeding, but even that doesn't seem to slow him down.

I'm a different story. Sweat plasters my shirt against my skin, and my knees and back are so stiff it feels like they can't bend again. But they do; I make them. Everything close is blurry, so I'm even more clumsy than usual. My hands get cut and my forearms scraped as I grip the rocks, but I keep going. If Tai can recover after a beating like that, I can't give up.

The other boys are almost as tired as we are, but we all keep going. By the time the sun sets, stones are piled high where the latrines will be built. The river pours water cleanly and quickly into the farmer's irrigation channels.

"At ease," orders U-Tha-Din finally, and we slump to

the ground, groaning. "Tomorrow we'll start construction. The work will be a bit easier."

The captain comes out from the barracks to inspect our work. He calls the sergeant over, and they speak in low voices. Then he walks to his jeep and climbs in.

I breathe a bit easier; maybe he's leaving camp for good. But U-Tha-Din beckons to Tai and me. His expression is annoyed. "Tough luck, boys," he says. "The captain wants to talk to you."

14

Tai and I make our way to the jeep while the others stumble to the gym. I swallow my fear as we approach the silent figure in the driver's seat. Tai moves forward to stand right beside the jeep. I feel a twinge of envy—what would it be like to feel so brave at a time like this?

"Did you think you'd get away with only a beating?" the captain asks Tai.

"No, sir," Tai answers.

"You're right. If you're to serve Burma, you must learn the meaning of obedience. There's always a few like you in every group. Come closer, Teacher."

I step forward, my eyes on the ground.

"What's the matter? You crying?"

I don't answer. Both my cheeks are tender to the touch from the smacks and kicks I received earlier.

He spits on the ground at my feet. "Do you hear me? Answer when I ask you a question."

"Ye-e-es, sir," I manage.

"The sergeant said you have some work for us, Captain," Tai says quickly.

"I do. Once everyone else in the camp is asleep, the two of you are to move that pile of stones back into the river. Right where they were before. Complete the job before morning. Without a word to anyone. Understand?"

I look up. Am I hearing right? I must be, because Tai looks as astounded as I am.

"But, sir," he says. "Ten recruits spent the whole day clearing the river. How can the two of us put the stones back before morning? And don't we need them to build the latrines?"

"Put those stones back. There's a small cell in our barracks for recruits who don't obey. The ceiling's so low you can't stand. If I hear that you didn't do the job, you'll each spend a week in there. Alone."

He turns on the engine and roars off into the night, leaving us staring hopelessly at each other. How can the two of us reverse a task that's taken so many an entire day to accomplish? And even if we manage to lug back all the stones, U-Tha-Din and the other recruits will be furious. And what will the farmer say? He asked us to complete the job by tomorrow. The whole camp will lose the promise of milk and eggs.

The captain's elite soldiers have lit a bonfire near the gym. "Have fun, boys," one calls as we walk off into the twilight. "Captain told us about your assignment. Don't go anywhere, now—it might be fun to hear the leopards enjoying a midnight snack."

They laugh as we head over to the pile of stones looming like a mountain in the darkness. I take a deep breath and stoop to pick up a stone. Might as well tackle the biggest ones while I still have energy from dinner. Before I collapse.

Tai is gazing off into the distance. "Hmmm," he says. I straighten and follow his line of vision. He's focused on a flickering light in the farmhouse window across the river. "You rest, Chiko," he tells me. "I'll be back soon."

"We have to get started, Tai. Where are you going? Didn't you hear what those guards said about leopards prowling out there?"

"I won't go into the jungle."

I shake my head. "Do you want another beating? You barely survived the last one."

Tai shrugs. "Half of that was acting. I'm an expert at beatings—I told you I'd teach you how. Don't worry. There's always an easier way."

He's gone, sprinting to the riverbank as if his bruised feet are starting their day. The darkness swallows him as he splashes away, and I'm alone. I turn back to the pile of rocks. How are we ever going to get this job done? Every bone and muscle in my body is aching. *Maybe I should rest for a few minutes*, I think. I can't help myself—I lean against the pile and close my eyes.

A rustling creak and a loud splash bring me to my feet with a start. I've been asleep, but for how long? Then I see it—a dark shape, growing as it approaches. What is that . . . that *thing*? Some animal from the jungle? Is this how I'm going to die? *Do something, you idiot! Call for help!*

But before I can cry out, Tai's voice comes through the darkness. "Chiko! It's me! Say hello to Yan and Gon."

I peer into the darkness, but I still can't make out exactly what's coming toward me. Why is Tai's voice coming from such a height? "What—?"

"I've got the farmer's two buffalo."

"How'd you manage that?" I ask, trying to register that the bulky monster is actually two large, docile water buffalo pulling a cart.

"I told him we needed them to complete his job by tomorrow. He grumbled a bit, but he agreed." Tai's teeth flash in the moonlight as he jumps off the cart.

We use the animals to pull the rocks across the field, but we still have to pile them into the cart. Each rock becomes harder and harder to lift, and Tai leaves again to scavenge in the construction site. "Go check on those guards," he tells me.

I tiptoe back until I see the silhouettes of the soldiers. They're flat on the ground, and I hear them snoring.

Tai has found a long plank. Resting it against the cart like a ramp, we roll and slide the biggest boulders along its length. The buffalo make short work of the distance across the field, and after only three trips, the job's done. The two of us—using the sturdy creatures, a plank, and the cart—have moved the stones back to the river in just a couple of hours.

After Tai returns the cart and buffalo to the farmer, we creep past the sleeping guards into the gym, change into our *longyi,* and slide under our blankets.

"What time is it?" I whisper.

"About midnight, I think."

"What will we tell U-Tha-Din in the morning?"

"Trust me," Tai murmurs sleepily.

I stay awake for a while, too tired to fall asleep. Beside me Tai snores lightly, and I remember back to when I first saw him. *Uneducated boy,* I thought then. *Who does that kid think he is?*

Tonight all the book learning in the world couldn't have helped me finish that impossible job on my own. Daw Widow was right. I do have a lot to learn.

15

A shout wakes us before the roosters begin crowing. "Everybody out! *Now!*"

We scramble into our uniforms and head outside. In the distance U-Tha-Din is pacing back and forth by the river. As we hurry to join him, the rest of our section starts to realize what has happened. The captain's soldiers are snickering at the sight of the rocks back in the river.

The sergeant glares at Tai and me. "Well?" he asks.

Tai and I exchange glances. *Speak up!* I tell myself, but I can't think of anything to say.

"The captain ordered Chiko and me to move the rocks back," Tai says. "So we did."

"*What? Why?*"

I flinch as the other recruits aim scowls and spit insults in our direction.

"Punishment," Tai says. "For trying to escape."

"Well, this is wonderful!" U-Tha-Din says sarcastically, beginning to pace again. His stocky figure reminds me of a caged boar I saw once in the zoo. "The captain is returning with a major later today. He told me that we have to dig out and haul *another* pile of rocks from the river this morning. Another pile as large as the one we *thought* we'd already moved. If we don't get both done in time, I'm finished. In fact, I'm finished now."

U-Tha-Din seems to have forgotten that he's an officer addressing a group of new recruits. Tai actually grins. I can't believe it. "Don't worry," he says. "Chiko and I have a plan."

U-Tha-Din stops pacing. "A plan? What plan? Come here, boy."

Tai talks to him in a low voice, and soon the sergeant is squinting across the river to the farm. When Tai is done explaining, U-Tha-Din claps Tai on the back. "It just might work!" the older man booms. "Go on, boy!"

It does work. With the cart, buffalo, and the same long plank, our section finishes the task before noon. Now two huge piles of stones mark the construction site. The freed

75

river pours smoothly downstream into the farmer's irrigation channels. When Tai returns the buffalo, the farmer is so delighted he sends along two dozen eggs, milk, and a pail of sugarcane juice.

"You've earned this, boys," U-Tha-Din tells us, beaming. "Nice work."

The other recruits cheer and clap Tai and me on the back. Sinking into the grass, we bask in the sunshine and share the sugarcane juice. Under the cooking tarp, the soldiers on kitchen duty start frying rice with egg.

"You did it!" I say to Tai, sipping the sweet juice slowly to make it last.

He doesn't seem happy, though. Instead he has a distant look in his eyes.

"Are you worried about what the captain will do when he finds out?" I ask.

"I don't really care," Tai mutters, banging his empty cup against the ground. "I need to get out of here. I asked the farmer for advice, but he has no transport either. Besides, he's scared of the captain, just like everybody else."

How can he still be thinking of escaping after what happened yesterday? "Maybe that truck driver made it back to Yangon," I say. "My mother has her letter by now if he did. Maybe she's trying to find Sawati."

Tai doesn't answer, but he smiles. I offer him some of my share of rice and egg, and he shakes his head. "You'll need your strength," he says. "Especially when Captain Evil comes back later to check on us."

While U-Tha-Din naps in the shade, the captain's soldiers organize our afternoon training. Win Min, irritated that we've somehow managed to outfox his "father," takes special pains to make us work hard. He's rigged an obstacle course and runs us through it six times. We do push-ups and chin-ups until my arms burn like two sticks on fire. After tea break it's time for kickboxing.

I've avoided being called forward for any matches up to now, but those guards have their eye on me, especially Win Min. Tai must realize the same thing. During the break, he takes me aside. "When one of them throws a kick at you, try to fling your head back hard before the kick lands and yell. Then fall to the ground before the full weight of the foot can ram into you. Once you're down, the match will be over. No harm in everybody thinking you're weak; it's better than being in pain, isn't it? Or dead?"

"I suppose," I say doubtfully.

"Let's try it," he insists. "We have a few minutes."

We slip behind a tree and act through his suggestion in slow motion, with me recoiling as soon as Tai's foot comes near my face. We only have time for two practice sessions, but I'm glad we manage even that, because Win Min calls my name first. Thankfully, Bindu volunteers to be my rival. The word among the recruits is that he doesn't kick very high or very hard.

The match begins. Concentrating hard, I hold my breath as Bindu's foot lands on my stomach. The others were right; he doesn't kick hard at all. I try to follow Tai's instructions as best I can. Before I know what's happened, I'm on the ground with Bindu grinning over me. He's won, of course, but I'm not in any more pain than I was when we started.

During dinner, I grin as Tai imitates my groans and moans. "Sounded like somebody was killing a pig," he says. "You sore?"

"Definitely. But not as much as I might have been without your training. And if those buffalo hadn't done our work, I'd probably be dead by now."

"Buffalo like to help each other," Tai says, nudging me. I laugh; he's pointing at U-Tha-Din, who's chewing his rice absentmindedly, looking just like Yan and Gon.

16

As camp begins to close down for the night, I watch the road. Tai may not care, but I do. What will the captain say when he finds out what we've done? I've almost convinced myself that he isn't going to show up when the jeep comes hurtling down the hill.

The inside of my mouth tastes like I've swallowed sawdust instead of fried rice. *One day at a time*, I tell myself. *Mind your own business. Stay out of trouble*.

Carrying kerosene lanterns, the soldiers run to open the doors of the jeep. The captain steps out, followed by his guest, a portly man with several ribbons on his uniform. We lower our heads to show respect.

"U-Tha-Din," barks the captain, after the bowing and saluting is over. "What kind of a leader are you? Why are the recruits not working? Have they cleared that river as the farmer requested? We must maintain good relations with that man. If not, the major will make sure somebody else is assigned to take over this camp."

U-Tha-Din grins broadly. "The work's on schedule, sir! The farmer already sent his first payment in gratitude for our work."

"*What?*"

Grabbing a lantern, the captain heads for the construction site. The major and U-Tha-Din stay behind, but everybody else follows the captain, with Tai at his heels and me at the rear of the procession.

Moonlight sparkles on the river. The captain stops short when he catches sight of the rocks piled in two huge mounds, just as he ordered. He studies the irrigation channels in the farmer's field. Then, in one swift motion, he turns and grabs Tai's collar, yanking him close. He's so angry, he's forgotten to keep up his fatherly façade. "Did you put the stones back into the river?" he growls. "All of them?"

Bindu steps forward. "We found them there this morning, sir. Isn't that right, boys?"

The captain lets go of Tai's collar. His voice is more

controlled this time. "Tell me exactly what happened."

Before anybody can answer, the major joins us, followed by a grinning U-Tha-Din. "I heard that two of your recruits managed a difficult task quite efficiently," the major says. "Where are those boys?"

The other recruits nudge and shove Tai and me forward. I catch Win Min's scowl in the crowd of faces.

"These boys borrowed a cart and two water buffalo, sir," says U-Tha-Din, his beady eyes gleaming. "They talked the farmer into the loan."

The major smiles and claps U-Tha-Din on the back. "Good work, Sergeant. The captain said you want to see action on the front lines, but I think we need you here."

U-Tha-Din beams even more brightly.

"Isn't that right, Captain?" asks the major.

"Yes, sir," the captain answers, but that muscle in his cheek twitches like a snake about to strike. "Soldiers dismissed."

The major heads back to the jeep, but the captain lingers. "Get ready for some time alone, street scum," he tells Tai. "And you, too, Teacher."

"It was my idea," Tai says quickly. "Chiko had nothing to do with it."

"Is that right, Teacher?" the captain asks, turning to me. "Should I punish your friend?"

I try to make myself speak, but nothing comes out of my mouth.

81

Tai answers for me. "I'm the one," he says, elbowing me out of the way.

With the major waiting, the captain doesn't have much time. He calls U-Tha-Din back and barks his orders. "Give the street boy three days of solitary. Starting immediately."

I wait for U-Tha-Din to protest, but he salutes his commanding officer.

It's done. Tai is going to confinement, and I'm not.

So why do I feel like the one who's condemned?

17

U-Tha-Din tells Tai to go to the gym and change out of his uniform. He places one hand on Tai's shoulder before walking away. I stay with Tai, trying to think of something to say.

Tai puts on his old *longyi*. "I'll be fine, Chiko. It's only three days. Two nights. Stay out of trouble while I'm gone."

That's my problem, I think. *I try to stay out of trouble.*

I can't meet his eyes.

Win Min and two other soldiers escort Tai to the confinement room behind the barracks. They don't let me follow; the place is off-limits to everybody except the captain's favorites.

Bindu is on guard in the gym, so I ask what the place is like. "It's a cell no bigger than a box," he tells me. "No windows and no bathroom. Just a hole in the ground."

The next day, I approach one of the captain's men with a kyat note and ask him to give Tai some of my food and water, along with a blanket. The soldier takes the money—snatches it, in fact—and agrees to the food and water, but refuses to give Tai the blanket.

For two nights I can't sleep. I toss and turn, hating myself more than ever, worrying that Tai is cold, or sick. How could I let him shoulder the blame for something we both did? Will I ever stop being a coward?

On the third day after dinner, Tai is released. He's weak but still upright. I'm waiting for him as he comes around the barracks. He even manages a smile when I rush to his side. I've brought his other *longyi* along and help him to the river so he can bathe.

I take his dirty clothes, go downstream a bit, and scrub them out while Tai washes himself from head to toe. Thank goodness it's time to sleep—he looks exhausted.

"I'm sorry, Tai," I say when we're finally settled in the gym. He's shivering, even though he's under his blanket, so I give him my blanket, too.

"For what?" he asks. "For not getting thrown in there with me? The stink was bad enough without you adding to it. And thanks for the food, Chiko. I'd be dead if it wasn't for you."

"How did you . . . ? What was it like?"

He's quiet for a minute. "I could hardly breathe. Not being able to stand was the hardest. I made it only by picturing Sawati's face."

"I'm sure she's with my mother, Tai."

But he shakes his head, unconvinced.

18

Tai's body recovers quickly, but the anxiety over his sister gets even more intense. No matter how hard he tries, he can't figure out a way to escape. Cars and trucks don't come now that the material for the latrines has been delivered. The dense jungle cuts us off from the rest of the world better than any wall or chain-link fence. Two or three of the captain's soldiers are on patrol at all times, showing off the new rifles only they are allowed to carry.

The camp has a small number of expensive foreign-made assault rifles that are assigned to "trustworthy fighters for Burma." And how does a soldier earn that label? Judging by the sections trained before ours, only a proven admirer of the captain's can handle that kind of weapon. The rest of us never come close— we're stuck with older, less reliable rifles made cheaply in Burma's factories.

Our own section is starting to divide into two groups also—a few boys who follow the captain's elite and the rest of us who don't. Tai is fast becoming the leader of the second group. His water buffalo maneuver and survival in solitary have earned respect.

U-Tha-Din, too, starts giving Tai more responsibility. We recruits continue to work at finishing the latrines, and the sergeant tells him to organize us at the beginning of the day.

"Nine of us working today," Tai says. "The rest are helping with rifle practice."

"Why don't we work in shifts?" I suggest. "Three of us can do the heavier work while three others measure, and three work with smaller tools. Then we'll switch. That way we won't get tired at the same time."

"Good idea, Chiko," Tai says. "But we need to keep track of the shifts to make sure everybody gets a turn to rest."

"If I had some paper, I could set up a system," I say.

"Did you hear that, Sergeant?" Tai calls. "Chiko could use some paper."

U-Tha-Din hands me his clipboard. "Tai tells me you can write, boy," he says. "Use this to figure out your system.

And while you're at it, why don't you take a look at some of these other letters? I'm—er—much too busy to do paperwork."

I like the feel of the clipboard and pencil in my hands. "I can't read and write without my glasses, sir," I say. "The captain told me not to wear them."

U-Tha-Din glances around. "Do you have them?"

"They're in the gym."

"As long as you don't wear them around the captain or any of his men, you'll be fine. These fellows won't say anything, right?"

The seven boys standing with us agree, and I race to get my glasses. I'm safe for now; the captain's soldiers are at the far end of the field, concentrating on shooting practice. Two recruits from our section are helping to set up targets.

I list the names and ages of the nine workers on the blank piece of paper attached to the clipboard. Dividing us into three groups, I balance the younger boys with the older ones. Although it seems like I'm ordering them around, the others don't mind. They see that my plan is fair.

When it's my group's turn to take a break, I pick up the clipboard and flip through the rest of its contents—several forms that haven't been completed, an unfinished budget report with a lot of math mistakes, and six unopened letters. Why would such important paperwork go untouched like this? Is the sergeant too busy to read his mail?

I walk over to U-Tha-Din, who's dozing in the shade. As I watch his face, the jowls shaking with each snore, the truth dawns—I'll bet the man can't read.

U-Tha-Din stirs and sits up. "What is it?"

"Do you want me to read these letters to you, sir?"

He looks at me suspiciously, but I keep my expression blank. "Good idea," he says. "My eyes get—er—tired from the sunshine. Another boy used to help me, but he's gone now."

"What happened to him?" I can't help asking.

"The captain sent him to the front lines."

I slit open the first envelope, noticing Tai and the other boy in our group watching. "Find something useful to do!" U-Tha-Din snaps, and they back off.

The first letter is from Yangon's military headquarters. It's a commendation about the negotiations U-Tha-Din arranged with the neighboring farmer. *Major Wang-De visited the camp and noted your leadership abilities. We have decided to raise your salary accordingly.*

U-Tha-Din is grinning. "You're a good reader, Chiko," he says. "That requires a thank-you note; put it in a 'reply required' pile."

The other letters are also from Yangon. One is the most interesting. It seems that our platoon's trained soldiers might be called out earlier than expected. They're needed to push back a "fierce tribal onslaught in the jungle." I think of Bindu's good-natured round face; we're always happy when he's assigned to train or guard us. How much longer will he be with us in the camp?

"They're making a big fuss over nothing," the sergeant scoffs. "Don't say anything to the other boys. No use worrying about things that might not happen. Is that it?"

"Yes, sir. Four of these require replies."

"That will take some time. It would be good if you did paperwork with me every now and then during the morning work sessions."

Extra time off from hard labor! What a gift Father gave when he taught me so well! I can only hope he's earned some special privileges, too. Wherever he is.

Suddenly a new thought hits me, and I can hardly breathe. Maybe I can use this assignment to find out about Father—to know for certain that he's alive! I might even be able to discover where he is and send Mother the news.

I hand the sergeant the clipboard and envelopes. "Here you go, sir," I say, trying to keep the excitement out of my voice.

19

The jeep careens down the hill in the evenings every other week or so. I'm grateful that the captain has to oversee other platoons so he can't stay for long, but I don't dread his visits as much as I used to. Each time he comes, he hands Win Min a pile of letters and papers. "For the sergeant," he says.

The sergeant catches my eye as he gets the mail. The size of this new stack promises me hours of escape from hard work. U-Tha-Din hands over the letters I've written, and the captain tosses the replies into the back of his jeep. Then he walks to where we're waiting in formation. I steady myself, waiting for more special attention.

But to my surprise, he ignores Tai and me altogether. Instead he addresses our entire platoon, with that fatherly smile fixed on his face. "I have a treat for you. We are going to watch a film in the gym. Soldiers and recruits both."

Most of the boys cheer, and we file into the gym. A sheet is pinned to one wall, and someone lights the lamps. We sit cross-legged on the floor, facing the sheet, while two soldiers bring in a film projector and a small generator. U-Tha-Din begins setting it up, muttering under his breath as he twirls buttons and knobs.

The captain is talking, making some of the boys laugh with small jokes and praising our hard work. His teeth gleam in the flickering lamplight.

"My sons," his deep voice says, "our country is putting her hopes into your hands. You, my dear ones, will lead our beloved country to peace and stability. We Burmese will return to school and college, travel abroad, make discoveries, and help make the world a better place for all countries. Our only obstacle is the rebel army—enemies and foreigners who care only about their own needs. Because of them, we waste time spending money on weapons instead of books. We waste time training soldiers instead of doctors and teachers. If we stop them, our motherland can move forward to join the ranks of other civilized nations."

Am I imagining it, or did his eyes linger on my face with the words *books* and *teachers*? A hunger to read is gnawing in a corner of my mind. Does he know it's there? And I can't keep my heart from leaping at the thought of living in a country at peace. What would that be like?

Behind us the sergeant is getting more and more flustered over the projector's wires and knobs.

"Hurry, U-Tha-Din! We're running out of time!" the captain barks. The change in his tone shatters the spell of his words—at least for me. Quickly he catches himself and calms his voice again. "Do any of our brave new soldiers have a plan to stop our enemies?"

Tai raises his hand.

I can't believe it. I want to dig my elbow into his side. Does he want to draw the captain's attention? Maybe he *likes* spending time in solitary and getting kicked. The other boys are as surprised as I am, and whispers travel around the room.

But the captain stays in propaganda mode. "The street boy has a desire to serve Burma," he says. "I noticed his leadership potential from the start. That's why I've been hardest on him during this training. Do you have an idea about how to stop the traitors, my son?"

"No, sir," says Tai, standing up.

"Then what do you want?"

U-Tha-Din has stopped fumbling with the projector and is staring at Tai.

"I want to watch the film you've brought us, sir," Tai says. Keeping his hands behind his back so that the captain can't seen them, Tai slaps the side of one fist into the other open palm.

"I do, too." The captain flicks a look of impatience at the sergeant.

Sheepishly, while everybody's still watching, U-Tha-Din responds to Tai's clue, picks up the power cord, and plugs the projector into the generator. A square of light flashes onto the screen. Everybody cheers.

Tai sits down. "Stupid buffalo," he mutters so that only I can hear. "I was trying to save him. He could have waited to plug it in when nobody was looking."

"Not everybody is as smart as you are," I whisper back. In fact, hardly anybody is. I think of Daw Widow—it's uncanny how much Tai reminds me of her.

"Nice work," the captain tells the sergeant in a mocking tone. "Start the movie."

Scenes of the Burmese countryside glow on the white sheet. Our national anthem plays. A woman's lilting voice describes how the "Kayah" and other tribes are "determined to destroy our foundation of stability and the hope for progress." Photos of brave Burmese soldiers flash on the sheet, cutting a path through the jungle, marching proudly over a bridge, standing at attention with rifles tilted at the same angle.

I almost—but not quite—manage to forget the captain's

presence. When the movie is over, he gives another flowery speech, repeating how proud he and the leaders of our country are of us.

Soldiers and recruits alike begin to cheer. Tai claps his hands loudly and slowly. I don't join in at all. I can tell by his narrowed eyes that the captain has noticed both Tai's fake zeal and my lack of it, but this time, he lets it go.

20

I have to make myself indispensable to U-Tha-Din to get information about Father. At first I write replies exactly as he dictates them. I obey so diligently that he heaps me with praises.

But after transcribing dozens of letters word for word, I pick a reply that's addressed to a childhood friend of the sergeant's—a friend stationed at army headquarters in Yangon. After dictating the letter, U-Tha-Din starts reminiscing about this buddy and their family connections. He doesn't notice me adding a postscript to the letter: *Can you find out where this prisoner is located?* I pencil in Father's full name, fold the letter, and seal it in the envelope while the sergeant is still talking.

I can hardly wait to get an answer about Father. Knowing he's alive will give me the courage to endure anything that's ahead.

Later that day I flex my biceps in front of Tai's face. "Take a look," I tell him, unable to keep the pride out of my voice. Is this the same spindly arm that waved goodbye to Lei in Yangon?

Tai takes a huge bite out of a juicy slice of papaya. "You'll be ready to take on Captain Evil in no time."

I shake my head. How can Tai talk lightly about a man like that? I never feel ready to face the captain; every day that passes without a visit from him is a gift. And Win Min and his cronies don't bother us much when the captain's not around.

"I hope a truck comes soon," Tai continues. "It's still the only way I'm going to get out of here." He pushes his face deep into the papaya rind to savor every last piece of the sweet, orange flesh.

"There has to be another way, Tai," I say. "Now that I'm scribing for the buffalo, let me see what I can find out."

"I promised Sawati, Chiko," Tai says, tossing the limp rind of the papaya aside. He digs into his bowl of rice and beans. "I've even got some money now. Several paychecks' worth."

The captain was telling the truth about one thing, at

least—the army *is* paying us a salary. Tai is taking his payments in cash, and I can only hope that my earnings are being sent to Mother, as I asked. I relish the thought of her using them to pay back our landlord or to buy fish at the market. Without me around to eat everything in sight, she'll be able to make my earnings go far and send some for Father, too.

My longing to see them is growing more intense as the weeks go by. And Lei's picture is an addiction. I've started carrying the photos in my pocket under my uniform; the button keeps them safe. Glancing over my shoulder, I see that Tai's still concentrating on his rice bowl. Carefully I slide Lei's picture out of my pocket and cup it in my palm, holding it at a distance because I don't have my glasses.

"Why do you always stare at that?" Tai asks suddenly, from right behind me.

I put Lei's photo away as fast as I can.

"Who is she? Your cousin?"

"A neighbor," I tell him, turning to my own rice bowl.

Tai and I are friends now, but it's too soon to show him how beautiful Lei is, or to reveal my hopes for the future. Do I even have a future? When this group of soldiers heads out to battle, we recruits will become soldiers in their place. Some will help U-Tha-Din run the camp. Others will join the captain to round up and train a new group of recruits. And then it will be our turn to run through the jungles with rifles, fighting tribal people.

"You look at another photo, too," Tai says. "Who is that?"

I take out the photo of Father. This one I can share.

Tai studies it for a while. "I don't remember my father at all," he says, handing it back. "He left just after Sawati was born. I like to believe he's a good man, like yours."

"I hope you meet him someday. And my mother."

"I hope Sawati is with her, Chiko."

"That does it," I say, making my tone sound irritated. "Do you *really* want to help your sister?"

Tai looks at me, surprised, and nods. Papaya juice is smeared around his mouth. In the fading twilight, his face looks younger than it usually does.

"You *have* to learn to read and write," I say. "I can teach you quite a bit, even in a short time. You'll get a better job in the city if you can read and write—you said so yourself."

Tai is silent. Then he says, "Can you start teaching me to read? We usually have some free time after training. And maybe more time after dinner, if I eat fast."

"You? Eat fast? Now *that's* going to be hard."

He grins as I pass him the last bit of rice in my bowl. I keep my slice of papaya—watching him relish his has made me hungry for mine. Once the rainy season ends, fruit will become scarce. Closing my eyes, I take a bite, letting the sweet juice fill every part of my mouth.

21

I filch bits of paper from the sergeant's clipboard for Tai's reading lessons. I still have the pencil stub I found in the gym, and for our first lesson I print the alphabet carefully on the back of an envelope. We're resting during the break after dinner, and not everybody around is safe. I can't risk wearing my glasses, but I know the shapes of the letters by heart.

As I write, a small group of boys gather around us. At first they're joking and laughing, but soon they're watching my fingers as intently as Tai. I notice Bindu gazing awestruck at the letters I form, his mouth open.

Tai's a quick learner, just as I hoped. By his third session, he's reviewing the first twenty characters. The novelty wears off, and the group around us dwindles to just one other boy—Bindu. This means the three of us can move to a quiet part of the field and I can slip on my glasses. Bindu and Tai take turns practicing, but Tai is learning at least twice as fast as Bindu. Bindu doesn't seem to care, though, and is happy each time he masters a new letter.

While we study, the recruits play cards, swap stories, or sing songs. One evening we hear the sound I've been dreading—the roar of a jeep careening through the jungle, growing louder by the minute.

"Captain Evil's back," Tai mutters.

I tuck my glasses away. We hide the scraps of paper and pencil and join the others in formation.

The jeep stops, and the captain climbs out. He's smiling, his arms wide open as though he wants to embrace all of us. As he walks up and down the rows, he pats his loyal recruits and soldiers on the shoulder. "You're dismissed, my son," he says, and the boy heads off to the gym or the barracks for the night.

Now the only ones left in formation are the rest of us. The boys the captain has given up on. His father act hasn't fooled us, and he knows it.

We lower our heads and salute as he passes through

our ranks. Tai does it smartly; I can almost see him clicking his heels together. I, too, manage a salute, but I can't keep my hand from shaking.

"Call that a salute, Teacher?" the captain snarls. "Show some respect."

I do it again, trying to steady my hand.

"Not good enough," he says. "Maybe a few days to yourself would help. Unless your friend here would like to take them for you again. What about it, street boy?"

"Yes, sir," Tai answers, as calmly as though he's being offered an extra helping of rice.

"No!" I say. "Don't send him there again. Sir."

The captain lifts a corner of his lip. "Why not? Should I send you, then?"

I don't answer. I can't. I'll never survive in that small space—I'll die or go mad.

"I'll give you a choice, Teacher," the captain tells me, holding out the bamboo stick. "Give your street friend a beating or he goes back into the cell."

"I'm sorry, sir?" I ask. Have I heard him right?

"Take the stick!" he says. "Take it and hit him. Hard."

I back away. "I . . . I can't."

"Then send him to solitary. It's your choice."

I throw a desperate look at Tai, who's moved slightly so he's behind the captain's back. He's trying to tell me something, and I glimpse his expression of total pain followed by a quick smile.

Suddenly I know what he's planning to do. I only hope I can play my part.

"I'll beat him, then," I say, taking the stick from the captain, who seems surprised.

I walk toward my friend, lifting the bamboo high, grateful for the remaining boys who circle us and block the captain's view. Even the sergeant adds his bulk to the game.

Swinging the stick through the air as hard as I can, I let the bamboo strike Tai's back—pulling back sharply just as I make contact. Tai slaps his own thigh hard with an open hand to add to the sound of impact. He shouts in pain, and his body recoils so convincingly that I'm worried I hit him too hard. But then I catch sight of his face and realize that my blow hasn't hurt a bit.

Don't let the captain see it land, I pray, and hit him again just as Bindu steps between the captain and me. It's not much more than a nudge, but the sound of Tai's slap and yell are as loud as if I've slammed him with all my might. The next blow comes with U-Tha-Din offering his round body as a shield between the captain and me.

Four times I wield the bamboo against my friend, easing the force of the blow just as the stick lands. The boys around us shout, hold their arms akimbo, and dart this way and that so the captain can't get a clear view. Each time I make contact, Tai slaps the side of his leg with a loud thwack, shrieks, falls, and writhes in agony. Each time he slowly, agonizingly, gets up again. Finally he falls to the ground facedown and is still.

"I think he's unconscious," I tell the captain, holding the stick aloft and pretending to be out of breath. "I must have hit him on the head by accident."

The captain yanks the stick out of my hand.

U-Tha-Din bends over Tai's body. "I'm sure the major will be interested to know that you've put the life of one of my smartest boys in danger. Recruits! Take your comrade to the river. I'll tend to him." Three boys lift Tai's limp body and carry him away.

The captain glares first at the sergeant and then at me. But there's nothing he can say. He stalks to his jeep and leaps in, and the car storms away.

At the river several of us inspect Tai's back. There's no sign of the beating, not even a bruise. Nobody in the captain's loyal cadre is nearby, so as soon as the jeep is gone, Tai starts leaping around in the shallows, splashing us, and laughing, and we join in.

22

The hot April days begin to blur into each other.
We spend the mornings repainting the outside of
the barracks before the rains come. Sometimes a
few of us are assigned to wash all the uniforms in
the river; other days we're sent to pick mango-
steen or jackfruit along the edges of the jungle.
Despite the heat, the afternoon running, climbing, and kickboxing gets easier as my body grows
stronger. When I manage to land a kick or two on
Win Min's jaw or skull, I'm taken aback by my
own satisfaction. *Careful, Chiko,* I warn myself.
You might start to like this.

During the daily break, Tai progresses from reading letters to recognizing short words to deciphering brief sentences. Bindu moves at a slower rate, but he's learning, too.

"The cow gives milk!" Tai reads triumphantly.

"Dog and spoon?" Bindu asks, when it's his turn.

"Dog and cat," Tai corrects him, and once again I savor the satisfaction of teaching somebody to read.

My system seems to be teaching the mechanics of reading, but I want to get our hands on a book. There's nothing like the sound of rustling pages as your eyes speed across the words. But there's no such luxury in camp.

Besides teaching Tai and Bindu, the only part of the day that gives me pleasure is the stolen time with the two dear photos in my pocket.

One night Tai falls asleep early, and I move closer to the kerosene lamp. Bindu's on guard, and he always lets me blow the light out myself. Lei's photo looks especially alluring in the flickering light. Somehow, in the glow of the cozy circle the lamp throws, it's easier to imagine that she and I are alone.

"She's pretty," says Tai's voice.

Hastily I tuck the picture into my pocket, fasten the button, and blow out the lamp.

"Do you like her, Chiko?" he asks.

Settling back down on my blanket, I don't answer.

I can hear Tai stretching out on his blanket beside me.

"Aha! Well, I hope I'm there for the wedding day. I'll get a good meal for once and stuff this empty tummy. . . ." He starts humming a love song that every Burmese teenager knows.

I snort. "What do you know about it, anyway?"

"You learn fast on the streets," Tai says, his voice getting serious.

"Oh." I try to change the subject. "What's it like, anyway, living on the streets?"

"Not so bad. People take care of us here and there, and Sawati . . ." His voice trails off. "I have to watch Sawati like a hawk because she's so pretty. Just like the girl in your photo, Chiko. Some older boys were eyeing Sawati for a while. . . . *Hoy!* I have to get to her!" His voice breaks suddenly.

I can hardly believe it. Tai is crying. A boy our age doesn't do that unless someone dies, and this tough kid isn't just any boy our age.

I don't know what to say. Suddenly the only thing I can think of is Mother's face. "I'm sure Sawati is in my house right now. Safe and alive."

I try to make my voice full of conviction. It might be true, after all. We can hope for the best, can't we?

I can tell he's trying to pull himself together. "Are you s-sure, Chiko?" he asks, but his voice is still shaky.

"I know my mother," I say. "By now she'll have taught Sawati how to make my favorite hot-and-sour soup."

Tai wipes his face with his shirt. "Ha! I can't picture my sister in a kitchen. She'd much rather learn how to kickbox than cook."

"So she's strong, Tai? See, you've taught her how to take care of herself. She won't forget that. She'll be all right."

He takes a deep breath. "I never had a brother," he says. "Who knew I'd find one here, of all places?"

A brother. Lei's the only one who guessed how much I wanted one when I was little. "Who knew?" I echo.

"My brother may not be much of a fighter, but he's a decent teacher. Or maybe it's that I'm such a great student."

I flick him lightly on the skull. "You still have to learn to write. It's not enough just to read."

"I will, Ko," Tai promises. I catch my breath—he's called me "older brother" for the first time.

After a while I hear even, sleeping breaths in the darkness. I stay awake, planning out another writing lesson like it's the most important job in the world.

23

On his next visit the captain focuses on a soldier who lied to the army about his mother's side of the family. The boy claimed that his grandparents were Burmese when they were really members of the Shan tribe.

Before administering the punishment, the captain dismisses all his loyal "sons" except three. Those that he sent away head into the gym for the extra refreshment he's brought with him—bottles of Indian cola from the black market.

The rest of us are ordered to stay and watch.

The captain hands his bamboo stick to the three elite soldiers, and they get to work.

I stand back, trying not to focus on the victim's face. Tai tells me later that the beating ended when the captain spat on the body of the "half breed" and climbed back into his jeep.

The boys who carried out the punishment swagger off, leaving the battered figure sprawled unconscious on the dirt. He's alive, but barely. A couple of his friends carry him away to take care of his wounds.

The captain's jeep disappears into the jungle.

"I hate that man," Tai says.

"Me, too," I say, but my voice is distracted—the captain brought letters to camp. I'm hoping desperately for an answer from U-Tha-Din's friend.

Later, when the sergeant hands me the stack of letters, I rifle through them quickly. The reply from his childhood friend is there! After reading the others, I open it, trying not to show U-Tha-Din my eagerness. I read the whole letter aloud, except for the last lines. I read those to myself, hardly believing what they say. *That prisoner is alive and well. We have found him to be an excellent medic and are using his skills when officers are injured in battle.*

I feel like leaping and shouting with joy. Father is alive! And he's using his wits and talents to stay that way. If only I could let Mother know!

"Why are you smiling like that?" U-Tha-Din asks. "My friend can't loan me the money. That's not good news."

"Oh, you'll find a loan, Sergeant. Should we start writing your answers?"

In the gym that night, I tell Tai the good news.

"Your father's smart, Ko," Tai says. "Just like his son."

"Now I have to find out where he is. And maybe we can use a letter to get some news about Sawati."

"How? Who keeps track of street kids?" He looks around. "Is there enough light to do some more writing practice?"

The only time Tai stops fretting about his sister is during our lessons. He keeps pressing for more writing time, more instruction, more practice.

"You studied for two hours today already, Tai," I say. "Your mind needs a rest. *I* need a rest."

He grabs my arm. "Can't you see? I'm doing this for her."

I twist out of his grip. "Okay, *okay!* There's enough light. Here—use the back of this envelope."

Tai studies so hard over the next few weeks that I decide it's time for a quiz. I lead him to an isolated corner of the field. Bindu follows, as usual. Monsoon rains have started, cooling the fields and making steam rise in the jungle, so we cluster under the sheltering leaves of a mango tree.

"Exam time," I announce, handing Tai one of the letters that U-Tha-Din asked me to throw away. "Part one: read this aloud."

Bindu draws closer, an eager expression on his face. Tai gulps and frowns at the typewritten words. "Dear Sar . . . Sir . . . ," he begins hesitantly.

I shake my head. "Sarj. . ."

"Dear Sergeant," he reads. "The cost of ma . . . materials for new uniforms is more than we can afford." He's reading faster, growing more confident with every word. "You must keep to your bud . . ."

"Budget," I say.

"Budget to operate the camp." There. He's done, and he looks up with a huge grin.

"Good work," I tell him. "You pass the reading section. But the exam's not over yet." I turn the paper over and hand him the pencil stub. "Part two: write a short letter of resignation from the army. We'll have to burn it later in the cooking fire, but it's good practice to write something you believe."

Tai clutches the stub, his tongue sticking out of a corner of his mouth. Bindu and I peer over his shoulders, watching him form large, careful letters. "Dear Captain Evil," I read out loud. "I quit. This army is bad. You are worse. Ko and I are taking your jeep. Tai."

My heart leaps—he's learned even faster than Lei.

"Excellent!" I tell him. There were a few spelling errors, but I could read and understand everything he wrote. "You pass with flying colors."

"Thanks to you, Teacher," Tai says simply.

The title is the same one the captain uses, but it sounds different. Coming from Tai, it's a badge of honor.

24

U-Tha-Din bursts into the gym. "Get up! Get up!" he bellows, trampling across the floor of blanketed boys. "The soldiers are gone!"

We wake, stumbling over each other in the semi-darkness. Rain is pelting the tin roof of the gym, and the clatter adds to our confusion.

"What?"

"Where are they?"

"I don't know how they vanished from the barracks without waking me," U-Tha-Din says, panting heavily. "I didn't hear a thing."

Tai and I exchange looks. The sergeant sleeps like

a boulder and snores like an elephant. But how did two-thirds of the platoon leave the camp without waking the rest of us? Why hadn't we heard the roar of the jeep?

The monsoon must have muffled their departure; I can barely hear U-Tha-Din's voice over the din on the roof even though he's shouting. And maybe the captain parked the jeep at a distance. He wanted to empty the majority of the camp in secret. But why?

Tai answers my unspoken question. "Wanted to shock us," he mutters by my ear. "To remind us who's in charge."

I remember the letter about the soldiers being called out early. So it hadn't been a mistake after all! What would happen to Bindu on the front lines? I try to convince myself that he'll do well as a fighter, but he's so slow to understand. Just yesterday he grinned toothily as he recognized the word "mother" that Tai was writing. Now he's gone, his reading lessons finished, probably forever. I hope the few words and letters I've given him keep him safe somehow.

"You recruits will take over the camp duties," U-Tha-Din is saying. "You're promoted to full-fledged soldiers now."

Will we be ordered to go into the city to round up new recruits? Tai and I can plan our escape, and . . . no. That won't happen. I remember that day clearly, although it seems like a lifetime ago. Only the captain's most trusted soldiers went with him. There's no way Tai or I would qualify for a trip to Yangon. Our section includes a few boys who are intensely loyal to the captain; they'll be the ones entrusted with any trip into the city.

"Chiko, stay here," the sergeant orders. "The rest of you go outside at once. Start making breakfast."

Once everybody is gone, he takes a letter from his pocket. "This is from headquarters. *He* must have left it on my cot. Read it, boy. I'm all shaken up." He mops his forehead with a handkerchief and hands me a sealed envelope marked *URGENT!*

"Why doesn't he read the letters before giving them to you?" I ask. Especially a sealed envelope marked *URGENT!* The captain is much too power hungry to let important letters like this one go unopened.

U-Tha-Din grunts. "Can't read. Rice farmers, both of us. Grew up together. He was a bully even then." The gym is still dark, so he lights one of the kerosene lamps. "Go on now. Read it." I put on my glasses and read the two lines typed on the page. *We need an office clerk immediately. Next week a truck will come for the boy who has been writing the letters.*

The note is signed by a major. *The boy writing the letters?* My heart begins to patter like the rain on the roof. That description could fit only one person in the camp—me!

U-Tha-Din is scowling at the kerosene flame. "Great," he says, blowing it out with a big puff. "I wonder who told him about you."

116

I'm going to Yangon! I'll be able to see Mother and Lei! I might even be able to find and visit Father.

U-Tha-Din keeps grumbling as we head for the door. "Now you'll leave, and who will read for me?"

A sudden thought squelches my joy. *What about Tai? But wait—*

"Sergeant," I say, "I've taught Tai. He can read for you."

"Can he read and write as well as you?" U-Tha-Din sounds suspicious. "He's smart, I'll admit, but he is a street boy, after all."

"He's not quite as good as I am," I answer truthfully. "But he could make sense of most of the letters you've been getting from Yangon. And answer them, too. Besides, he'll get better with practice."

"All right, all right," U-Tha-Din says, still sounding grumpy. "I'll try him out later. Now get out there and take your place with the others."

I give him back the letter.

"Chiko," the sergeant calls after me, "don't say anything yet about your leaving. I don't want any jealousy or fighting in camp."

I walk to the cooking area in a daze, picturing Mother's expression when she sees me standing on the doorstep, her happy tears when she hears the news about Father, Daw Widow's shout of welcome, Lei's shy smile. . . .

The other recruits are under the tarp where the soldiers

used to gather. I join them, avoiding Tai's searching glance. How can I tell him *I'm* getting what *he* wants most in the entire world—a trip back to Yangon? I try to reassure myself—I'll promise to find Sawati and send word back to him. Mother and I will take care of her. Tai is bound to be happy for me; he's that kind of a friend, I'm sure of it.

After the shock of the soldiers' departure wears off, a festive mood fills the camp. Most of the recruits are excited that now we're the ones to sleep in the barracks on real cots, not on the gym floor, and that some of us might get to start practicing with newer assault rifles soon. Best of all, there's a lot more food for each of us.

The sergeant divides up the previous soldiers' tasks—cooking, cleaning, patrolling, drilling. He orders Tai and me to organize the afternoon training sessions. "I don't want the boys to lose the strength and muscle they've gained," he warns. "Make the practices as tough as the ones you've been having."

Tai and a couple of others run off in the rain to gather milk and eggs from the farmer, supplies that will seem abundant now that two-thirds of the camp has left. Another boy begins rummaging through the box of pots and pans and pulling out bowls. U-Tha-Din tells me to light the cooking fire, but the only box of matches I can find is wet. I strike match after match, with no success.

Tai and the others return with the food. Tai ducks under the tarp and shakes himself until water is no longer streaming from his clothes. Then he comes to stand beside me. "What did the buffalo want with you in the gym?" he asks.

The rain is slanting under the canopy and wetting the wood. I try to light another soggy match and groan in frustration. "He got a letter. I read it for him. I told him you could read, too, by the way."

"Why? He didn't need to know that."

"He asked," I say. "Besides, you should be proud. A boy who can read is getting rare in Burma these days."

"Reading doesn't help you do everything, Ko," Tai answers, taking the box of matches from me. He has a fire blazing in two minutes flat.

25

I watch anxiously as U-Tha-Din and Tai sit cross-legged in the shade. Tai's back is to me as he bends over a sheet of paper, but I see U-Tha-Din's appreciative grin and the way he claps Tai on the shoulder.

The sergeant gestures for me to join them. "Tai's quicker with numbers than you are," he tells me. "But you can certainly teach, Chiko. If you weren't leaving, I'd ask you to teach the whole camp to read."

Tai looks up, startled. "Leaving? Who's leaving?"

Idiot! Buffalo! I scowl at U-Tha-Din. *After he ordered me not to tell anybody. . . .*

The sergeant stands up hastily, avoiding my glare. "Have to check on the others."

"What's he talking about, Ko?" Tai asks, getting to his feet.

Here it is, the moment I've been dreading. *A truck's coming in a few days to take me back to Yangon,* I practice silently. I take a deep breath and open my mouth, but before I can answer, we hear a familiar sound coming down the hill.

It's the roar of an engine. A jeep engine.

Tai pulls my glasses off my face and hands them to me. I shove them into my pocket as we scramble into assembly, forming the familiar 3–3–4.

The captain brings the jeep to a halt, switches off the engine, and leaps out before the tires roll to a complete stop. "We need an extra soldier for a special mission," he announces. "A clever boy who can move quickly through the jungle. Do I have a volunteer? Who wants to fight for Burma?"

Nobody moves. Panic begins to squeeze into my throat, and I swallow hard to keep the salty taste of it out of my mouth.

"I'll have to choose somebody, then." The captain strides through our section, row by row. I hold my breath and concentrate on the ground. His pace slows in front of me, but to my relief, the boots keep marching. Before I can exhale, though, they come to a stop.

He's standing in front of Tai.

He's placing a heavy hand on Tai's shoulder.

Tai's wiry body always straightens defiantly in the captain's presence, and I wait for it to happen again. But this time he seems to slump, and my heart sinks.

"Since there are no volunteers," the captain says, "I pick you, street boy."

Memories play on the screen of my mind like scenes from a film. Tai stepping out from the canvas of the truck so that I wouldn't be punished. Riding the water buffalo toward me. Teaching me to handle a beating. Frowning in concentration to make the shapes of a letter. Stepping up to take my punishment. Grieving beside me in the darkness. And calling me "Ko" since that night.

No! I tell myself. *Think of Mother. You're her only son.*

"We leave now." The captain yanks Tai out of line, shoving him toward the jeep.

Tai throws me a look over his shoulder, and for the first time I see fear on his face. I touch my pocket. *You could be home by tomorrow, Chiko. You've only known this boy a few months. You can't risk your life for him. Mind your own business. Stay out of trouble.*

But the voice in my head made a mistake by bringing up that mantra. With a jolt, I realize that this really isn't about Tai at all.

It's about me.

If I keep listening to that chant in my head, I'll stay alive, but what kind of a life will it be? I want to live a life worthy of our family name.

If only I wasn't trembling from head to toe like bamboo in the wind. Straightening my shoulders, I breathe a prayer. *Give me courage.*

As though someone has pulled a plug, fear drains from my heart like water from a basin. I leave my place and walk over to the sergeant. The captain doesn't notice; he's too intent on shoving Tai toward the jeep. "Send Tai to Yangon instead of me," I whisper in U-Tha-Din's ear. "He can do that job. I'll go with the captain, come back, and keep reading your letters."

U-Tha-Din's mouth falls open. He studies my face. Slowly he nods.

I stride over just as the captain throws Tai into the jeep and grab my enemy by the shoulder. The captain whirls, scowls, and pulls out of my grasp.

"What do *you* want, Teacher?" he asks, sneering.

U-Tha-Din has followed me, but he doesn't say anything. Everyone else is as still as the boulders in the river, watching, waiting. Tai sits in the back of the jeep, staring in shock.

"Tai has another assignment," I announce. "The major wants him in Yangon. I'll go on your special mission."

There. It's done.

"I'm taking the street boy," the captain answers, but he's measuring the expression on my face. "Get back in formation before I lose my patience."

I don't flinch, and I suddenly realize how much I've grown since arriving at the camp. I'm now almost as tall as he is.

"Take me with you," I say, moving a step closer. "Tai is going back to Yangon. Major's orders."

Tai's mouth is opening and closing like a fish's.

"What is this job in Yangon, U-Tha-Din?" the captain barks.

"The major needs a boy who can read and write," U-Tha-Din answers. "A truck will be coming to pick Tai up sometime in the next few days."

I hear murmurs of surprise from the other recruits. Tai's head swivels, and he gapes at U-Tha-Din.

The captain spits on the ground at my feet. "Read? That stupid street boy? Never!"

"He can read," I say. "And write. I taught him."

U-Tha-Din smirks and holds up the letter. "Want to read the order yourself? Or you could ask Tai to do it." He's enjoying the chance to shame the captain.

The captain grabs my collar. "You! Thinking you're better than other people. You prideful, arrogant—"

"Take me with you instead of Tai," I say again, twisting from his grip. The training exercises have paid off; I'm much stronger than I was a few months ago.

124

Tai's mouth finally cooperates with his desire to speak. "You can't do this, Ko! I won't let you!"

Tai's protest convinces the captain. "Get out of that jeep, street scum," he barks, opening the door. "*You* don't have a choice. All right, Teacher. Maybe you are the right one for this mission."

He pulls Tai out, and I grab my friend's hand. "Visit my mother," I say. "Tell her I'm coming home soon. Tell her about Father."

"But—but—," Tai is still spluttering.

The captain shoves me into Tai's place. Hard. "No time for good-byes. Let's go!" With one last scowl of distaste at Tai and U-Tha-Din, he climbs into the jeep and turns on the engine.

"Should I get my things?" Thankfully, my two most important possessions are already in my pocket, along with my glasses and a few kyats.

"You won't need them," he says, slamming his foot on the accelerator.

I fall backward with a thud but manage to turn as we roar up the hill.

My last sight of the camp is Tai, shouting and running behind us until we pick up speed and disappear into the jungle.

26

The jeep hurtles along the dirt road. The captain smokes one cigarette after another, scattering a line of discarded butts almost as though he's leaving a trail for somebody.

I sit quietly, relishing the sensation of not being afraid of him for the first time. We travel for a few miles on the road and stop as the sky begins to darken. The captain jumps out and pushes through the undergrowth and vines. I follow until we reach a clearing beside the river. Four soldiers are gathered around the warm glow of an open fire. They stand, bow, and salute.

The captain doesn't acknowledge the gesture. He grunts instead and heads downriver alone, into the darkness. Soon I see the red tip of yet another cigarette glowing in the distance.

One of the soldiers comes bounding over. It's Bindu, and he throws his arms around me in a bear hug. "I was hoping it would be you," he says. "Captain told us he was bringing a recruit."

We join the other three boys beside the fire. They're all on the unwritten but well-known list of the captain's most expendable soldiers—the ones he thinks are least loyal. I notice they're armed with new assault rifles, though.

"Look!" Bindu says proudly, pointing to the stock of his weapon. He's scratched the letters of his name there, and in the firelight I can see that he's done it right.

"Nice work, Bindu. Do you know how to shoot it?"

"Not really," Bindu answers. "We only got them yesterday. But he says we'll need them for the mission, and they're not too different from the old ones."

"Mission?" I ask. "What mission?"

"Don't know."

"It's time to find out," comes a voice from behind me. The captain must have finished his cigarette. "You'll be heading out first thing in the morning."

"Where are we going, sir?" one of the others asks.

"What are we supposed to do?" Bindu adds.

"Shut up and listen. A group of rebels has been stock-piling a stash of weapons in a hut across the border. Your mission is to spy out the cache and return with news so that we can send troops in to claim the weapons for Burma."

"How do we get there?" Bindu asks.

"I told you to listen, didn't I? You'll start in the morning and walk along the river for most of the day, but stay on the trail—it should be clear of mines until you cross the bridge into Thai territory. You'll have to camp somewhere because you won't reach the bridge by nightfall. Cross the bridge, and once you reach a spring, look for a side trail veering to the left, into the teak trees. That's supposed to be a shortcut, but if you don't see it, keep to the main trail and look for the next left-hand split. Take that, and soon you'll reach the hut."

"What then?" Bindu asks.

Slam! The captain's hand meets Bindu's face with such force that my own face aches in sympathy. Bindu is dazed, rubbing his cheek where the blow fell.

"Any more interruptions?" the captain asks.

Nobody answers.

"Once you get there, your job is easy: stay hidden, estimate the number of weapons and rebel soldiers, and bring back the news. Be careful and be smart, boys. Kill any rebels you see along the way. Except for you, Teacher, because I'm out of weapons."

I don't respond. I wouldn't know what to do with one of those complicated new rifles anyway. Is he disappointed by my lack of protest? Can he sense his loss of power? His expression is hard to read in the firelight.

"If you're captured, get as much information as you can and escape," he says. "If nobody gets back, we'll assume you failed, and another team will be sent to do the job. But I hope all of you return—the army will reward you well. And for an extra bonus, one of you has agreed to give me a full report of this mission. I won't tell which one; you'll have to figure that out for yourselves."

The other boys glance around suspiciously. Who has agreed to be the captain's informer? It can't be Bindu. He's neither crafty nor mean enough to agree to something like that. And they know it can't be me. Or do they?

The captain smirks at our reaction. "Always watch for traitors, boys. I have one last instruction. The teacher will walk first, ahead of the rest of you. I don't want to lose any trained soldiers to mines."

So that's why he needed Tai. It's my job to be a mine clearer. Still, I don't react. With a shrug, he turns and heads back to the jeep, and we watch him disappear into the darkness.

27

We start our mission at dawn. At first the captain's directions are easy to follow, and I jog ahead of the other boys, following the path along the river. I've lived with fear ever since the day they took Father; it feels wonderful to be free of it. At first I almost feel like singing as sunlight streams through the canopy of leaves and sparkles on the water.

But the morning wanes, monsoon clouds cover the sun, and the air thickens. Trot, march, trudge, slog. The captain didn't give us food, so we have to forage for bananas and mangoes along the path. I try not to think of the taste of rice, fish, eggs, anything other than fruit. I try not to worry.

By late afternoon my legs are tired, my shirt is drenched with sweat, and I'm sick of the whine of mosquitoes. Fighting hard to keep my spirits up, I imagine Tai knocking on my mother's door and finding his sister. I picture him starting an office job. And each time we stop for a rest, I slide Lei's or Father's face from my pocket and cup it in my hand so the others can't see it.

Once it gets dark we settle ourselves for the night beneath an old teak tree. Dinner is the extra mango or banana we're each carrying, and somehow Bindu manages to light a small fire so we can roast the bananas. We don't talk much—everybody's tired and hungry. Before long it starts to rain, and our fire sputters and dies. We fall asleep huddled together under the broad teak leaves.

The next morning it doesn't take us long to reach a rickety footbridge spanning the river and cross into Thailand. I start walking more cautiously now. I can almost hear Father's deep voice in my head. *Being brave doesn't give you license to be stupid, Chiko.* I'm still not too worried about detonating land mines—not yet, anyway. This part of the path is well used; it shouldn't have anything buried along or beside it. I'm thinking more of wild animals—leopards and cobras and other creatures. Or people who might leap out at any moment to ambush us. I'm starting to miss that rifle now—if only I had some kind of weapon.

At first the other four, even Bindu, keep a safe distance from me, trying to step in the footsteps I'm leaving in the mud. They walk in a tight pack, aware that the enemy might be lurking around any corner, or that a mine might explode under my feet. After a while, though, when nothing happens, they get careless again and catch up.

By the time we reach the spring, the main trail has dwindled into a slim, muddy line that keeps disappearing under vines and leaves. In the slippery circle around the spring, we stop to get our bearings. Bindu shares his canteen with me and squats beside the water to refill it. The other three start arguing about which direction we're supposed to be heading.

I spot a bamboo pole in the sunshine beside the spring. One end is carved into a sharp point, just like the captain's. The pole will give me a better chance of survival if we meet wild beasts or rebels. I'm glad the others are too distracted by their argument to notice me picking it up. The bamboo feels warm and alive in my hands.

"Captain said to find a trail heading left at the spring," I say, pointing into the dense teak trees. Broken branches block the view. "I don't see anything."

"Go look for it, then," says one of the boys. "It's almost noon. I want to get back across the border as soon as we can."

Another one chimes in. "We won't be able to count the cache in the dark."

I scan the dense leaves around the broken branches. A mine could be anywhere in there. "Let's stay on the main trail," I say. "We'll keep an eye out for the first clear path to the left."

They complain for a bit, but agree. We walk for a while and then round a bend. Almost immediately the main trail disappears into a thicket of brambles and trees and tall weeds. To the left is a wide, sunny field and to the front and right is a wall of prickly foliage. There's no sign of any trail—the main one or a fork.

"What now, Teacher?"

"Maybe we should go back to the spring," I say.

Another boy shakes his head. "This field slopes up to a ridge. We might be able to see the trail from up there, or even spot the hut."

"The field doesn't look safe," I say. "What if I push through the bushes straight ahead? Maybe the main trail keeps going beyond these brambles."

"Good idea, Chiko," Bindu says.

The other boys aren't happy with this. "If you don't get back in ten minutes, we'll go through the field."

Leaving them grumbling and arguing, I venture into the tangle, stepping carefully. It does look like the trail leads through this mess—I notice small crosses carved into the trunks of some of the trees. I'm watching for the markings and pushing my way through thorns and brambles a few minutes later when I hear it.

BAM!

It's the loudest crash I've ever heard in my life, so loud it almost drowns out the screams and shouts. My companions must have detonated a mine! Why didn't they stay where they were? I take a few steps in the direction of the noise.

BOOM!

This explosion sounds even louder than the first. The ground and the air and the bushes are on fire around me. I'm falling, howling, crashing into thorns and brambles. The last thing I remember is the bamboo slipping out of my grasp as I land with a thud.

PART TWO

TU REH

1

The sun is high and shadows are small when we stop to rest near a small spring. It's only the second day of the journey, but after walking for five hours straight, I'm glad to put down my load.

I wish we could have brought my mule along, but we wouldn't be able to hide her if we ran into trouble. It was a miracle that we brought her safely from our village to the refugee camp. Mango's a good little beast. Sa Reh promised to take care of her while I'm gone, but I can't help missing her as my pack gets heavier by the moment.

I replenish my water supply, and Peh points into a teak grove. "That's the way to the healer's hut," he tells us.

He hasn't put down his load to fill his canteen. Neither have the other men. They're used to trekking through the jungle with big loads for weeks.

"What healer?" I ask. It's my first mission. I've been asking questions nonstop.

"Two sisters live in a hut with their grandfather," Peh answers, handing me my pack. "People in hiding go there for treatment."

"The younger girl used to come into camp for supplies," another man adds. "She's a tough one—makes her way there alone, loads her bag, and heads back again the same day. They say her sister was captured and tortured by the enemy."

"Shh!" Peh says suddenly. "Listen!"

I strain to hear past the twitter of birds, the trickle of water, the drone of insects. Are those voices? Is that the tramp of boots?

It must be, because Peh pulls me into the trees. "Soldiers," he hisses.

Every muscle in my body tightens with anger. Those Burmese will stop at nothing. They kill without remorse—that's why our village had to evacuate three months ago. Most of the villagers hid in the jungle on the Burmese side of the border, but a few escaped into Thailand, like my family. I grabbed Mango and followed Peh and Mua and my sister. None of them turned around. They didn't see the soldiers burning our home and bamboo grove. But I did. My mind blazes with the memory.

"Get down," Peh orders now.

We obey instantly, flattening ourselves under the bushes and camouflaging each other with leaves. I reach out one hand and quickly cover the hem of Peh's trousers and his boot.

"Good work, son," Peh whispers.

I can't help feeling pleased, despite the danger. It's been a while since I've heard praise from either of my parents. Lately it's been lectures from Mua and disappointed looks from Peh. In fact, the entire camp was surprised when he chose me to be a member of the team, but I know why I'm here. I overheard my parents talking when they thought I was asleep. As usual, I was staring into the darkness, remembering the soldiers who burned our house.

"The boy's changed," Peh said. "He's full of anger."

"It's that new friend of his," Mua whispered. "He's a bad influence."

"You're right. Maybe it would be good for Tu Reh to join me on the next mission."

I almost jumped up and shouted, "Yes, Peh!" before remembering I was supposed to be asleep. I'd been wanting to join Peh's team since we got to camp. I was tired of wasting time with school and chores and games with my little sister while other Karenni fought to stay alive in the jungle.

"But it's dangerous," said Mua.

"He's sixteen now, my love, becoming a man."

"I know." Mua sighed.

"But what kind of a man is he becoming?" Peh asked, and he sounded worried. I could hear him crunching on the bamboo shoots Mua fries and stores as snacks.

"A brave one, like his *peh*," Mua said. "With a big appetite like his *peh's*."

My parents laughed. I saw Peh reach over and take Mua in his arms. One of them blew out the candle, and darkness hid them.

I don't care why my parents let me come. I'm here now, with Sa Reh so jealous he can hardly stand it. My parents were right about him and me being angry. He hates the Burmese as much as I do, maybe even more. When he was small they forced his *mua* into hard labor. She wasn't strong enough to survive it. Sa Reh once told me about the day they captured her. He hasn't talked about it to anyone else.

"Kill a soldier for my *mua*," he told me before I left.

I made the promise, but our mission on this journey isn't to fight. We're carrying medical supplies and food to Karenni hiding in the jungle. We don't even have any weapons. Peh said our camp needed to reserve them for direct combat.

The voices and footsteps are distinct now, closer, louder. Soon I see them through the leaves—five soldiers wearing that forest green uniform I remember so well. I lie quietly, barely daring to breathe. Have these soldiers already discovered some of our people, maybe even killed them? I picture myself leaping out at them, knocking down one, then two, then three. If only one of us had a rifle!

They're talking about finding the healer's hut and destroying it. My heart beats faster as I think of the two Karenni girls who live there with their grandfather.

Somebody has to defend them! I'm sure Peh is thinking like I am.

Five of us. Five of them.

We can take them, rifles or no rifles. I'm strong—my thighs and arms are as big as Peh's now. I brace myself, ready to leap out as soon as he gives the signal.

2

But Peh keeps still.

The soldiers have found the spring. Now they're only about twenty meters away, arguing as they fill their water bottles.

With a pang, I remember I didn't pick up my bamboo pole before Peh pulled me away. Will the soldiers find it? Will they feel the grip of my hand, still warm, on the bamboo?

They're moving again, marching, tramping, talking in loud voices.

Peh waits until we can't hear them before crawling out of the leaves. "Back to the spring," he orders curtly.

He and the others talk in low voices while I hunt for my pole. That piece of bamboo and Mango are the only two possessions I still have from our village. The pole is nowhere in sight. I cut it from the grove that was planted by my grandfather's father—the grove that is gone now.

BAM!

An explosion shatters the jungle. My hands fly to cover my ears. Not many things scare me, but detonating a hidden mine is one of them. Too many people in camp have only one leg.

When the noise stops echoing, Peh shakes his head. "Sounds like a claymore. That's the worst kind."

BOOM!

Another one! This one isn't as loud. For once I'm glad the Burmese planted so many mines in these jungles. If only more of them would explode under their own feet. It would make things so much easier for us.

"Let's get out of here," says one of the men. "If any of those soldiers are still alive, they'll be coming back this way soon."

"No, they won't," Peh says. "Didn't you hear what they said? They're heading to destroy the healer's hut and return by nightfall."

The other men are shaking their heads. "We'll have to fight those scoundrels if we follow them," one says. "We didn't bring any weapons, and we've got people waiting for supplies."

"The girls and their grandfather are in danger," Peh says. "Someone has to warn them."

Nobody answers, and none of them meet his eyes. I clench my fists. Isn't there a man on this team besides Peh?

"I'll do it," I say. If I leave my pack, I can run fast. I'll go through the jungle to pass the soldiers without them seeing me, warn the healer, and then race back here to catch up with the team.

Peh's expression doesn't change much, but I can tell he's pleased. "I'll show you a shortcut, Tu Reh," he says. "But first let's check on those soldiers. Will the rest of you wait?"

"We'll wait," someone answers. "We can't do this mission without you, Oo Reh. But hurry back."

"I will," Peh promises, and the men seem satisfied.

I leave my pack with them and follow my father.

3

We backtrack around a bend where the trail seems to end in a tangle of bushes. We just came this way, pushing through the undergrowth, so Peh and I know the main trail is just on the other side.

"What's that?" I ask, pointing into the field beside us.

Peh squints into the afternoon sun. A short distance away, four limp piles of uniforms are strewn across the field. The bodies don't move, but we keep still just in case and watch for a few minutes.

Peh takes off his pack. "Stay here, Tu Reh," he whispers.

I watch him make his way to the bodies. Why did these soldiers leave the trail? Uncharted land is peppered with mines. It's stupid to try to take shortcuts into the unknown.

Peh examines each soldier in turn, removing rifles from their bodies and gathering ammunition from their bags. They must be dead. That's good news. Those four won't kill or hurt Karenni again. The healer is out of danger, the girls are safe, and now we can take these weapons along.

Peh slings the four rifles over one shoulder and heads for the undergrowth bordering the field. I hold my breath each time his foot lands, but there's no explosion. He gestures to me and disappears.

Reluctantly I walk into the brambles and bushes. It's stifling in there. Small crosses are scratched on the trunks of trees to mark the cleared trail, and I keep a careful eye on them.

"A claymore killed the four on the field," Peh says when I come into sight. He's off the trail, but only by a few meters. "This one stepped on a makeshift mine. He's still alive."

A body is sprawled at Peh's feet. One leg is bent at a strange angle, but the chest is rising and falling with ragged breaths. I glimpse the splintered bone of shin poking through a shredded pant leg. If this soldier survives, which is doubtful, he'll lose that leg for sure.

Beside him is my bamboo pole—I recognize it immediately. A dark stain on the ground under the injured leg is spreading. I step carefully to where Peh is standing and grab my pole before it gets bloody.

There's no sign of a weapon. This soldier must not have been carrying one. I do spot a pair of eyeglasses not far from his head. I pick those up, too, and shove them into my pocket.

Peh hands me the ammunition and slings the rifles across my shoulder one by one. Once I'm loaded up, he scoops the Burmese soldier into his arms. What's he doing? This soldier isn't a danger to the people in the healer's hut. We can leave him to his fate, return to the team, and finish the mission.

"Make a path for me, Tu Reh," Peh says. "Time is short."

I shift the weight of the rifles on my shoulder and push my way through the brambles. As I hold back branches so Peh can pass, I wonder if he's planning to end this soldier's pain with a bullet. It would be like him to show that kind of mercy to an enemy. But why not do it back there? Why not end it quickly?

When we reach the open trail, Peh lowers the soldier to the ground and digs through his pack for his water bottle, ointment, and strips of clean cotton. Now I really don't understand. Why is he wasting medicine and supplies we brought for the Karenni on an enemy?

I watch in amazement as Peh washes the wound, applies ointment, and ties a tourniquet around the soldier's thigh. Then he wraps the leg with bandages to staunch the bleeding. Finally he rises. He places his fingers on the soldier's wrist. "He might still live."

"He's *Burmese*," I say, the frustration ringing in my voice. "Why are we helping him, Peh?"

"He's hurt badly. The animals will tear him to pieces tonight."

"Then we should end his pain now," I say, handing Peh one of the rifles. "It's loaded. I checked."

Slowly Peh takes the rifle. "We could do that," he says. "But there's another choice."

"What?"

"We could carry him to the healer's hut."

Was I hearing right? "No, Peh! We promised the men we'd go back."

"I made that promise, Tu Reh," Peh says. "You didn't."

My heart sinks. What's he saying? What does he want me to do?

Peh reaches for my bamboo pole, and I give it to him. He holds it in one hand and the rifle in his other. It looks almost like he's weighing them.

"A man full of hatred is like a gun, my son," Peh says. "He can be used for only one purpose—to kill."

I know. That's what I want to do, what I've dreamed of constantly since we escaped—making the Burmese pay.

Peh hands the rifle to me. Then, with a swift flick of his wrist, he tosses the bamboo pole high in the air. It's light, so it rises easily and arcs and falls without a sound.

We each catch an end. "The rifles are good, Peh. You're glad we have them, aren't you?"

"I am glad. I'm not denying that. It's a find, four rifles and ammunition, too. But could you kill a wild animal with this bamboo, Tu Reh?"

"Yes, Peh."

He knew I could. I fought off a wild pig once. The animal raced right at my sister, and I beat it so badly we cooked it the next day. But I've also hunted with rifles, and so has Peh.

"What else can you do with it, Tu Reh? Do you remember harvesting it?"

We're still holding the bamboo like a bridge. I picture our beautiful grove dancing in the sunlight and the wind, and for a second it's hard to answer. "Mua cooks it," I manage at last.

"She uses it for fuel, too, remember?"

"And we make medicine out of it. Baskets. Houses. Rafts. So many, many things."

"That's right. And that's why I'm going to stay like the bamboo, Tu Reh. I want to be used for many purposes. Not just one."

Peh releases his end of the pole, and it lands on the ground with a thud. "I won't command you, my son. A Karenni man must decide for himself. Leave him for the animals. End his life now. Or carry him to the healer. It's your choice."

4

I feel dizzy. How can Peh leave this to me?

"Don't decide too quickly, my son," Peh adds. "Take some time to think." He picks up his pack and the other three rifles and walks around the bend, leaving me with the soldier, the fourth rifle, and my pole.

I have both weapons in my hands. I can use either one. It's my choice, he said. But even though I can't see Peh, it's like he's still there. And I know what he wants me to do. I know how he feels about killing someone—he sees it only as a defense, a last resort.

I carry on the argument with him in my head. If I carry this soldier to the healer's hut, it's going to take me too long to get back. I'll never catch up with the team. No! *I want to take this journey with you, Peh. The whole journey.* I've pictured our return to camp with stories to tell of Karenni lives we saved. Sa Reh will be so impressed. How can I give that up after only a couple of days, all because of a stupid Burmese soldier? Why couldn't he have died like the others?

The fire rages in my head. *Leave him here, Tu Reh. He's Burmese. A soldier. They're destroying our people, our land, our future.* Leopards or wild dogs will pick up the scent of blood. They'll tear him to pieces by nightfall.

I turn to go. But the soldier is stirring. He moans. One hand gropes for the pocket on his shirt.

I can't help glancing at his face. Beads of sweat gleam on his hairless upper lip. He can't be much older than fourteen or fifteen. Just a kid, really. Could I leave a boy younger than me to be attacked by beasts? It's a terrible way to die.

The flaming voice in my head answers so loudly I'm surprised Peh doesn't come running to shut it up. *Then kill him yourself! Use the weapon they were carrying to kill us!*

It's time to act—time to grow up and become a man. A man for the Karenni.

I fling down the bamboo pole and lift the rifle. Placing the stock against my shoulder, I aim the barrel straight at the soldier's skull.

Do it! Kill him!

But as my fingers tighten around the trigger, the boy's eyes open. They stare into mine. He says something in a low voice, repeating the same word again and again.

I hear it.

I understand it.

This boy wants his mother.

Mua's face, lined with worry, comes whirling into my mind. Somewhere, far away in the plains of Burma, another mother is waiting for a son to come home.

I swear.

I lower the rifle.

He'll die anyway! Kill him!

The voice isn't done shouting, but I can't obey it.

Not with those eyes staring at me; not with that voice calling for his mother.

I sling the rifle back on my shoulder and pick up the bamboo pole. "Peh!" I call.

Peh comes hurrying back. He scans the soldier from head to toe. I see the relief in his face. "Still alive," he says.

"Probably not for long," I answer. "But I'll try to take him to the healer."

Peh doesn't hold back his proud smile. "That's good, Tu Reh."

"What should I do when I get there, Peh? Should I stay and protect the girls and their grandfather? Won't other soldiers come and try to rescue this one?"

Peh places both hands on my shoulders. I try not to show my surprise, but we both know that fathers only do this once or twice in a son's lifetime. We stand face-to-face for a long moment. "One decision leads to another, my son. God will show you the way."

5

I put down the rifle and tie the canteen and my pole securely to the loops on my trousers. When Peh lifts the boy and places him on my back, I stagger before steadying myself. The boy's arms dangle limply, and I clutch his clammy wrists. The smell of sweat and blood and maybe something worse attacks my nose.

Peh slings his pack and all four rifles over his shoulders. He leads me into the teak grove to find the trail. At least I won't have to cut through the jungle now that the other soldiers are dead. He lifts and kicks fallen branches and other debris out of the way until we see a trail veering up to the left. "When you get to a broken tree, look to the west for the hut. Shouldn't take you more than two hours if you keep moving. I'll see you back in camp in a few weeks, Tu Reh. And trust me, you'll be the first man I pick for the next mission."

Giving me a quick smile, Peh's gone. I want to shout after him, *What's next? Tell me what to do, Peh!* But instead I turn and start trudging up the hill. My first task is to get to the healer's hut. Will we make it before dark?

The Burmese boy is thin, but heavy in his sleep. I lift and place each of my feet slowly on the trail, drawing on every ounce of muscle in my legs. Soon, too soon, I have to rest. I lower the soldier to the ground with a thud. The boy moans in pain, and his eyes open again. He tries to speak, but this time no sound comes from his dry, cracked lips.

I unbuckle my canteen, still full from the spring, and drink deeply. What's wrong with me? I can't kill this enemy; I can't even leave him for the animals. *Gone soft,* Sa Reh will say, if I ever tell him about this crazy turn of events. Maybe the soldier will do me a favor and die on the way. Deserves it, the idiot, for leaving the trail.

I sit for a few minutes more and worry. I'm bringing an enemy to the healer's hut. How can I be sure they'll receive him? And even if they do, I can't leave him there. Other soldiers are sure to come searching for him. The girls and their grandfather will be trapped and captured, perhaps even killed. We'll have to flee for camp as soon as we can. And *then* what to do with the Burmese boy?

Blast this soldier. Why has he crossed my path?

Those eyes are watching me again. They flicker to my canteen.

Blast him again, he's thirsty. I sigh, reach over, angle the canteen, and let some water dribble into his open mouth. The boy swallows again and again before sinking back into sleep.

The sun is low in the western sky. Mosquitoes swarm around us, lured by the taste of blood and the scent of sweat. With a grunt, I heave the boy onto my back and trudge forward, step by tired step.

It's twilight when I finally reach the broken tree. Beyond it to the west is a mound of green vines and leaves. A gust of wind shifts the vines, and I catch sight of a small bamboo hut camouflaged under the greenery.

The soldier is unconscious again, his blood seeping through Peh's bandages. I leave him by the tree and head for the hut.

A voice rings out. "Stop!" it commands. "There are mines everywhere. Please wait there."

A girl about my age comes into sight. She's wearing a black tunic and white sash, like other Karenni girls, but hers don't have any of the usual red or green tassels sewn on them. She moves quickly across the ground, almost hidden in the shadows, weaving to avoid the hidden killers that must surround the house.

As she gets closer I see a long braid of hair swinging

behind her. She might be pretty if she were smiling, but it's hard to tell with that tough expression on her face.

"Can I help you?" she asks.

"I've brought a wounded boy. Shattered his leg on a mine."

"Where is he?"

"Back at the tree."

"Get him inside, quickly. I'll show you where to step."

She's bossy, but to the point. I like that. It makes it easier to tell the truth. "He's a soldier. A Burmese."

The girl's gaze meets mine. "Bring him," she orders. "I'll tell my sister to get ready."

6

Inside the hut, lighted wicks float in two cans of kerosene. An older girl is waiting beside a clean sheet spread across a mat made of soft grass. She beckons, and I lower the boy onto the mat.

"Careful," the younger girl says. "His leg's bleeding again."

"That's why he's here," I respond curtly. I'm tired.

An old man sits cross-legged on a mat, about to eat rice. The air smells of turmeric and ginger, and my stomach rumbles loudly.

"Hungry?" the younger girl asks, smiling for the first time. She *is* pretty. "Wash up first."

Pretty, but bossy.

I shrug; I haven't eaten since the morning. The girl leads me to a bucket of water on the back stoop. "The river's that way," she tells me, tipping her head toward the jungle behind the house. "In case you want to take a bath tomorrow."

I probably smell. I should wash up, but I'm exhausted. "Where's the privy?"

"Over there. But hurry. Grandfather's waiting to eat with you."

"Can't he tend the soldier first?" I ask, annoyed. "I dragged him all the way here—"

"My sister's the healer."

I'm so surprised I forget to speak quietly. "How can *she* be a healer? She's too young."

"She learned while she was with them. One of the Burmese soldiers was a doctor, trained in England, and he taught her." She bends, squinting into the darkness by the door, and plucks a chili pepper off a bush.

"An *enemy* taught her to heal?"

"Crazy, isn't it? But that's not what she says."

"What does she say?"

"That God can bring beauty and goodness from anything."

I can't believe it. "Has she talked about what happened to her?"

She hesitates, and when she speaks, her voice is low

and shaky. "No, she hasn't. Not yet, anyway. I hope—I pray she will someday." Then she tosses her braid over her shoulder. "Go on, use the toilet."

I stalk behind the hut and find the small outhouse near a grove of papaya trees. I'm fighting another choking wave of anger. I know what Burmese soldiers do to Karenni girls. We all know.

The girl hands me a sliver of soap when I get back. "I'm Ree Meh, by the way," she says. "What's your name?"

"Tu Reh."

"Staying in the camp or the jungle?" She pours water over my hands.

"Camp. They let us in because my father's a leader in the resistance." I can't keep the pride out of my voice.

"I didn't see you when I visited last winter."

"Got there three months ago." Anger makes me barrel the next words at her, even though she's not to blame. "They burned our village. Soldiers. Like the ones that took your sister. Just like that fool I dragged here."

"They burned ours years ago," she says, but her voice stays steady this time. She hands me a clean cloth. "Here, dry your hands. Now let's see if we can fill that talkative stomach of yours."

Ree Meh locks and bolts the door behind us with a loud snap and click. The soldier's eyes fly open. They search the dimness of the hut until they rest on the older girl's face. Then, to my amazement, the soldier smiles. He murmurs something I can't hear. The healer keeps working without a word.

I can't help looking closely at her. Her hair is pinned back, and there's a scar across one cheek. Is the sight of this soldier bringing back memories? But there's no trace of disgust as her hands steadily remove the bandages.

The girls' grandfather smiles, patting the place beside him. He's so old he can probably remember the days before the British left and Burma took over. There aren't too many veterans of that war alive; even Peh was born after we were annexed. I'd like to ask him how it was back then, what it felt like to have our own country, but that's going to have to wait. First we need a plan.

Ree Meh pours me a cup of coconut milk. "I hope my sister can keep him alive," she says. "He lost a lot of blood."

"She has to work fast," I reply. "He was heading this way with four other soldiers. They're dead, but it won't be long till more come."

"Let's give him a chance first," the old man says. "Put some of my granddaughter's good cooking in your stomach while you wait."

Ree Meh ladles rice and curry made of bamboo shoots on a tin plate. The grandfather is already chewing with gusto.

The food looks good. I start eating.

7

The old man doesn't want to make any plans until the healer's finished. "We have to know how the boy is faring," he says.

It seems like hours before she's done. Ree Meh quietly cleans and orders the hut. Her grandfather sits in silence. I pace the room, stopping every now and then at the window to listen. Only the sounds of the jungle are out there, noises I've heard since I was a child. I grip my bamboo pole tighter. I have to protect these girls and their grandfather. That's my new mission.

Finally the healer places both hands on the boy's

chest and bows her head. The hut stays silent until the soldier stirs and opens his eyes.

This time he's fully conscious. One hand reaches to clasp the pocket of his shirt; the other gropes for his leg. "Is it there?" he asks in Burmese. "I can't feel it."

"I pray you keep it, my brother," the healer answers. It's the first I've heard her speak. Her voice sounds like music, even making the ugly sounds of Burmese.

"The pain's gone," he says.

"I've given you medicine for that. But I think . . . I think you may lose it."

The boy takes a deep breath before speaking. "The whole leg?"

"You'll keep your knee. It's the part below it and the foot. I've splinted it and stitched it up, but it might still get infected."

The healer turns to me. "Is Auntie Doctor in your camp now?"

I shrug. "Yes. She's with us for a bit longer, I think."

Even though Auntie Doctor's getting older, she still travels from camp to camp half the year. The rest of the time she's based in a clinic in the largest camp, treating people who trek for miles to get help. Amputating torn limbs and fitting prosthetic replacements are a big part of her job.

"I've been wanting to meet her," the healer says. "They say her healing is as good as her heart." She and her sister start putting away the unused bandages and medicine.

The old man squats beside the soldier. "What were you doing on the Thai side of the border, young man?" He's fluent in the boy's language. The Burmese government and military make sure most of us understand enough to obey orders.

The boy clears his throat before he answers. "Our captain sent us on a mission. We were supposed to find a Karenni hut full of weapons."

"But there is no such place around here," Ree Meh says, also speaking Burmese.

"His crew was heading here," I say. In Karenni. "It's the only hut around for miles. I'm sure more soldiers will be sent to find it. We have to get to camp."

The girls exchange glances. "Will they let us stay there?" Ree Meh asks. "Space is so tight."

"I'm sure they will," I answer. The Thai government puts a limit on the number of us who can live inside the camp, but our council reserves a few precious spaces for emergencies. Well, this is an emergency, isn't it?

"Will they let the soldier in, too?"

What? I can't believe she's asking this. "Absolutely not," I say. "They'll think he's a spy. Sent to find where people are hiding. To discover plans. To identify leaders. In fact, how do we know he *isn't* a spy?"

I'm still speaking our language—Sa Reh and I swore

164

we'd never let a word of Burmese come out of our mouths. Not until we have our own country back and every last one of the intruders is outside our borders.

"He's not a spy," says Ree Meh, speaking to me in Karenni again. "He's just a boy."

"He's a soldier," I say, and I can't keep the stick in my hand from pounding the floor. "We leave him here."

"The camp council might let him in," Ree Meh says. "He wasn't carrying a weapon, right?"

"This one wasn't, but the others were. Besides, I don't trust any of them." I'm sure the leaders will agree with me, especially the ones who train our defenders, like Sa Reh's father.

"He won't be able to do much spying with his leg torn up like that," Ree Meh says. "No weapon and an injury—they can't turn him away."

I stand up. "We're not going to take him along! I'm telling you, they won't let him in. Besides, if the Burmese find the dead bodies back there, and then this empty hut, they'll think we've taken this one hostage. They'll come after us. They might even overtake us."

"He needs to get to a doctor fast," Ree Meh says, lifting her chin.

"His leg is sure to get infected if we leave him, Tu Reh," the healer adds. "That wound needs to be cleaned and treated, and his bandages changed. The soldiers who come probably won't know how to do that."

"They'll have to learn how," I say. "Let the Burmese doctors take care of their own."

Ree Meh's arms are folded across her body. So are mine. The healer looks from her sister to me. "Grandfather must make the decision," she says finally.

The three of us turn to the old man. Once again he squats beside the soldier. "Any medics in your training center?" he asks.

The boy shakes his head. "No, sir."

The grandfather stands and eyeballs me, long and hard, before he speaks. "We take the Burmese boy with us," he says.

I can't hide my frustration, and my pole smacks the ground again. No wonder we're losing this war!

The soldier calls out something.

"What, my brother?" the healer answers, hurrying to his side. I wish she'd stop calling him that.

"Where's the boy who carried me here?" he's asking.

Ree Meh takes hold of my sleeve and pulls me over. "Here he is," she says. "His name's Tu Reh. What's yours?"

"I'm Chiko."

The healer taps herself. "Nya Meh," she says. "And that's Ree Meh, my little sister. Although the way she bosses me around, you'd never guess it."

The boy manages a smile, his eyes traveling from my face to the girls and back again. "You saved my life," he says. "How can I repay you?"

"Be well," the healer says, tucking the sheet around his chin. She's as gentle as if he really were a brother.

He takes her hand. "My mother says there's a special glow that marks a healer. I used to think that was an old wives' tale, but I saw it on your face. You remind me of my father. He's a doctor—a healer, like you."

"Me? I have so much to learn," Nya Meh says.

Ree Meh brings the soldier a glass of the same kind of coconut milk she poured for me. "Hungry?" she asks him.

He shakes his head no. "Maybe in the morning," he says, and drinks the milk.

I go to the window and open it again, leaning out to listen. Were they marching through the night? Would they get here before we left?

After they eat and wash, the girls spread their mats in a corner of the hut and hang a shawl across the room. Talking to each other in low voices, they disappear behind the homemade curtain.

I walk to the Burmese boy and lean close to his ear. "Repay them by staying here," I tell him, breaking yet another promise to Sa Reh by speaking the enemy language. "You put all our lives in danger if we take you along. Tell the old man in the morning."

The boy's eyes widen, but he nods.

I spread out on a mat near the grandfather and try to sleep.

8

In the dim, dark green light of dawn, I walk to the privy, keeping my eyes on the branches of the tall teak trees, where mud-colored snakes like to slither.

When I get back, the girls and their grandfather are packing clothes, pots, pans, tools, and medicine into bags. The soldier is still sleeping.

"Tu Reh, will you cut two bamboo poles for me?" Nya Meh asks.

"Yes," I say. There's something about the way she asks a question that makes it hard to say no. But why does she want bamboo?

168

"Please make them about the same length and width," she says. "There are nice ones by the river."

"I'll come with you," Ree Meh says, frowning. "Because of the mines."

I can, however, say no to this sister. "I'll go alone, thanks. I know how to find a marked path."

Thickets of bamboo line the river, but the light, strong branches are easy to cut. Deer graze nearby. They stare at me with startled eyes.

I bring the bamboo back, and Ree Meh ties four corners of an old blanket securely to the two poles to make a stretcher. "Our grandmother wove this cloth," she says. "It's tough enough to lift a horse."

"I wish we had my mule here," I say, eyeing the large packs waiting to be carried.

"You have an animal?" Ree Meh asks.

"The only one in camp," I say. "She carried my sister all the way from home."

The soldier is awake. He needs to go to the bathroom. "Will you take him, Tu Reh?" the healer asks.

I'm impatient to get on our way, but I agree, hoping she won't ask for a cloud or something. I'd probably jump as high as I could to try and get it. And it isn't because she's a girl and I'm a boy. It's the same thing that makes it so easy to obey Peh. They make you *want* to help them.

We manage to get the boy up on one foot, and he

loops an arm around my shoulder. He winces as he hops to the privy.

On the way back he stops me and says quietly, "You're right about me putting you in danger. I'll stay, Tu Reh."

Is he trying to trick me? I look closely at his face, but he's concentrating hard on every step. I can tell he's in more pain than he was last night. He's breathing hard when we reach the old man. "Leave me here, sir," he says. "I can care for my leg. Nya Meh will show me how."

"No, my son," the grandfather replies. "You've never seen an infection taking over. You won't be able to think straight. You could die."

"Listen to him, please, Grandfather," I urge. "They'll come after us."

The old man lifts his chin, reminding me of his younger granddaughter. "Take the Bible out of my pack, Ree Meh. Turn to the book of Ecclesiastes. You know the passage."

Long ago, when people brought the Holy Book here, most of our ancestors learned it in Burmese. Now we're translating it into Karenni, but the old ones still know most of it by heart in our enemy's language. The grandfather mutters along as Ree Meh reads the words aloud:

There is a right time for everything:
A time to be born, a time to die;
A time to plant, a time to harvest;

170

A time to kill, a time to heal;
A time to destroy, a time to rebuild;
A time to cry, a time to laugh;
A time to grieve, a time to dance;
A time for scattering stones, a time for gathering stones;
A time to embrace, a time to refrain from embracing;
A time to find, a time to lose;
A time for keeping, a time for throwing away;
A time to tear, a time to repair;
A time to be silent, a time to speak;
A time for loving, a time for hating;
A time for war, a time for peace.

Old habits are hard to break. Peh and Mua like us to stand silently for a minute after a reading, letting the words settle into our minds and hearts. It seems that the girls grew up with the same practice, because they're also silent.

I know the words the old man intended me to hear: *a time to kill, a time to heal.* Will there ever be a time for me to kill? What about to defend and protect? We don't even have a weapon handy in case we need it on the way to camp.

The soldier kept his eyes on the old man during the reading. "It's not the right time to take me with you," he says, breaking the silence. "I'll put your lives in danger."

"We need to get you to camp," Nya Meh tells him as

she ties the top of her pack closed. "The doctor there can amputate; I can't."

Again the soldier spreads a palm across the pocket of his shirt. What's in there that's so precious?

"Let's go, Tu Reh," the old man says. I want to keep arguing, but he gives me such a stern look that I know I have to obey him.

The girls and I move the soldier to the stretcher. Once he's settled I take his glasses from my pocket and toss them onto his lap. "Here. These must be yours."

The soldier's face lights up like fireworks as he grabs for the glasses. "This is the second time I've lost them since I left home! A thousand thanks, Tu Reh."

He puts them on. One lens is cracked, but it doesn't seem to bother him. I can't help noticing that his grin looks like my sister's when I whittle her something or tell a good joke.

"We have to hurry," I say, turning away.

9

Ree Meh stoops to grab the bamboo poles on one end of the stretcher, and I bend to take hold of the other end.

"One, two, three!" Nya Meh calls, and we lift on three, somehow keeping the stretcher fairly flat. Ree Meh is strong; the boy doesn't feel heavy with the load shared like this.

Nya Meh lifts the blanket and checks his leg. "It looks okay, Chiko," she tells him. "The splint is holding, and so are the stitches."

The soldier doesn't answer. He's fallen back into an exhausted sleep, one hand still over his pocket.

Nya Meh holds the door open, and Ree Meh and I carry the stretcher out of the hut. "They'll probably burn everything," Ree Meh says, swiveling her head to take one last look at the place she's been calling home.

"You didn't build it, right?"

"No. And it wasn't built well." But I can see her profile. Her eyes scan the chili pepper and tomato plants, the papaya trees, the bamboo-shaded path to the river behind the hut.

The old man comes out last and bolts the door. I can't believe what he's carrying along with his pack.

It's an assault rifle.

And he's got ammunition slung across his chest.

Plenty of it.

I'd clap my hands if I weren't holding the stretcher. I'm ready to fight to the death to defend him and the girls, but it's good to know I'll have some backup.

The grandfather trots nimbly through the hidden mines to where we're waiting. "There's a right time for everything, my boy," he says, noticing my close look at the rifle. "A Karenni man must decide for himself when to kill."

It's almost exactly what Peh told me. Did schools used to teach sayings like that in the old days?

We get on our way. It helps that both Ree Meh and I know the trail well. After an hour or so, we're moving like one unit, our steps keeping perfect time. Her braid swishes in front of me like Mango's tail.

Marching, marching, marching, never slowing, never stopping. Biting flies buzz around our heads, branches snap beneath our feet, the endless crackle of leaves. Shadows shorten and then lengthen as the sun moves overhead.

Nya Meh is carrying a heavy pack, but she's managing to keep up. When the trail widens, she walks beside the boy to keep an eye on him. Even the old man is moving at a quick pace, bringing up the rear. I'm glad he's back there with his rifle.

The soldier, although jostled with our steps, is still fast asleep. Soon, though, Nya Meh tells us he's burning with fever. She takes off his glasses and places a wet cloth on his eyes.

"I'll hold the specs," I say, and she tucks them into my pocket.

We keep moving, stopping briefly every now and then to listen. Ree Meh doesn't complain when I don't put down the stretcher to rest. We have to get to the river bordering the camp—Burmese soldiers don't dare to cross it, thanks to the defense of our camp patrol. That's why we hoard the few weapons we have. But we'll never make it there by nightfall, not at this pace. We'll have to sleep one night in the jungle.

By the evening, clean, cool raindrops begin to fall, and we tip our heads back to catch them on our tongues. As the water slides down my thirsty throat, I can't help noticing the soldier shivering on the stretcher. After all this trouble, is he going to die anyway?

We leave the trail and make camp in a small clearing. The ground is damp and hard, covered with slippery teak leaves and small stones. Ree Meh and I start to gather wood, but her grandfather stops us. "They'll see a fire or smell it," he says.

The night grows darker as we eat dried fish and papaya, trees rustling as unseen creatures catch our scent. Peh taught me to recognize the high-pitched cry of a hungry leopard, and I hear one in the distance. Fire would keep the animal predators away, but the old man is right. It could also lure people.

10

"His skin is darkening around the wound," Nya Meh tells us after a quick inspection of the soldier's leg by candlelight. I hear the anxiety in her voice. "Not a good sign. If only we could walk through the night. The doctor *will* be there, right?"

"She was in camp when we left," I say. "We should get there tomorrow afternoon if we keep up this pace."

"Get some sleep, sister," Ree Meh says. "If he takes a turn for the worse, I'll wake you."

The grandfather is already asleep, one hand gripping the rifle even as he snores.

I sit between Ree Meh and the sleeping soldier.

"You should rest, Tu Reh," she says. "I'll be fine."

This girl has lost a lot, too, like Sa Reh. And she's tough. I like talking to her.

"Can't sleep," I say.

"Why not?"

"Memories. But I guess we all have some. At least those of us who haven't grown up inside a prison."

"Prison?"

"Camp feels like a prison to me. Some people our age have spent their whole lives there—they're forgetting our homeland. Our country."

"Can you blame them? Camp life is all they know."

"You're right, but it's still hard. I hope we're not losing our desire to fight. We're getting soft, I tell you. We do stupid things, like bringing this boy along."

In the moonlight I see the chin lift that runs in the family. "My grandfather's not soft," she says. "He's fought hard to help our people. He's a hero."

"I'm sure he is, but do you think the Burmese would do something like this for us? Ha!"

"Well, then doing things like this is a good way to stay Karenni!"

Our voices have risen. "Be still, you two," the old man hisses. "Your sister needs her rest."

We're silent for a while, and then I hear Ree Meh sigh.

"What's wrong now?" I ask.

"Nothing."

"Why the sigh, then?"

"You've got me worried about moving into camp, Tu Reh. Are . . . are there many girls who've grown up there? I didn't see many our age the last time I was there."

"They were probably in school. There are lots of them."

"Those girls. Are they anything like me?"

What kind of crazy question is this? We're in danger, escaping through the jungle, and she's worrying about the other girls in the camp?

"Not really," I answer. "You're different."

It's the truth. Most girls my age make me feel clumsy and rough, like a boar smashing through the jungle. I usually keep my distance. But Ree Meh isn't like that. It doesn't feel like I'll crush her.

"I'm different?"

"Definitely," I answer.

"That's what happens when you grow up without a mother," she says, and I hear a new wistfulness in her voice.

"No, no," I say, mad at myself for not making it clearer. "That's not it."

"Well, then, why am I different?"

"I don't know. You're . . . stronger, Ree Meh. More . . . more like a boy. Yes, that's it. You're more like a boy."

She flings her braid over her shoulder. "A boy?" she asks. "You think I'm like a boy?"

Somewhere in the conversation, I've made a terrible mistake. "No, no. Not like a boy at all. I mean—" It's too hard to explain.

"Granddaughter!" It's the old man, and I realize our voices have gotten louder again. "Come and rest. Tu Reh can watch alone."

Without another word she gets up and strides away.

I smile and lean against the trunk of the teak tree. I like this tough, sweet girl. She's a fighter.

For the first time in a long time, the night isn't full of angry memories. Instead I daydream myself into the future. A twenty-year-old Tu Reh is building a strong hut shaded by a bamboo grove, planting rice paddies, fishing on a bridge.

And wait! Who's that?

There she is—a girl with a glossy black braid and warm brown eyes, planting a chili pepper bush beside the hut.

She's probably trying to boss that future me around. But I think he likes it.

11

The ground shakes me awake. I've fallen into such a deep sleep that I have no idea where I am. Leaping to my feet, I glance around in a daze.

Another tremor makes the earth move and the trees quiver.

And another.

The girls and their grandfather are up almost as quickly as I am, the old man with his rifle leveled and ready. "Elephant!" he shouts. "Get behind the tree! Bring the boy!"

Ree Meh and I race to the stretcher. The soldier moans as we lift him but doesn't wake. His bandages are drenched with blood, and his leg below the knee is oozing with pus and looks twice as large as normal. Nya Meh throws it a worried look as we lug him behind the biggest teak tree, where she and the old man are already hiding.

Again the earth trembles under our feet, but this time it doesn't stop. A wild, booming call echoes through the jungle. And then we see him—an enraged bull elephant, blood pouring from a gash across his leg.

He tosses his huge head from side to side, bellowing.

He's headed straight for our tree.

The curve of sharp tusks gleams in the sunlight.

The girls are shouting, shoulder to shoulder, blocking the path to the injured boy. The grandfather stands next to them with his rifle ready.

I move out from behind the tree and yank the bamboo pole off my belt.

"Get out of the way, boy!" the grandfather bawls. "I'm going to shoot!"

A bullet or two won't keep this beast from trampling everything in his path. Peh told me once that only a frontal attack can frighten an elephant off.

Wielding my pole like a spear, I race toward the elephant, yelling at the top of my lungs.

The big creature screeches to a four-footed stop. He's startled, already threatened because of the fresh wound on his leg.

"YAAAA!" I shout, and lunge at him again.

His eyes survey me, my pole, my stance. And then he decides to turn. His massive, wrinkled sides heave with the effort of it. Bamboo trees crash and are smashed to pieces under his feet.

With one last roar of rage, the huge animal thunders back up the trail.

We're breathing heavily, sweat pouring down every face.

Except the soldier. He's missed the whole episode, muttering in his sleep, that one hand still protecting his pocket as though his heart itself were in there.

"Tu Reh, thank you," Nya Meh says. "You risked your life for us. For all of us."

"Your parents raised you well, boy," the grandfather says. "I'll tell them when we meet."

Ree Meh says nothing, but her smile makes me feel like I could scare off a hundred wild elephants.

And then we hear it.

A shout in the distance, somewhere on the trail behind us.

Someone else is about to encounter our fierce attacker. Someone calling for help from his companions. I can't make out all the words, but I hear enough to know it's Burmese.

We're being followed.

12

The elephant becomes our defender, keeping our pursuers back, buying us time.

Without a word we pick up our loads and move as fast as we can, listening for every crackle and sound behind us.

Minutes pass. An hour.

We keep going.

We're getting closer to camp, and they haven't caught up yet.

Maybe we'll make it.

We manage to stay together until the trail narrows and starts cutting back and forth downhill. The way leading to the river is overgrown with underbrush. The camp leaders like to keep it that way as an extra defense. It's hard to maneuver the stretcher now, and Nya Meh and the old man pull ahead.

Again we hear it—a shout. This time the Burmese words aimed at us are loud and clear: "Stop or we'll shoot!"

We move even faster. A bullet flies in our direction through the trees, followed by another. They're gaining ground. A third bullet smashes into the trunk of a tree close to the grandfather's shoulder.

"Run ahead!" I call to him and Nya Meh. "Warn the patrol!"

Nya Meh takes one last look at her sister's face and disappears into the brush. But the old man turns and comes toward me. He slings his rifle over my shoulder. "It's loaded," he tells me, and then he's broadening the path for us as he goes, tearing away as much of the growth as possible with his hard, old hands.

Ree Meh's doing her best to pull the stretcher through the overhanging vines and prickly undergrowth. I'm pushing and trying to keep it level. We're so close to the river—it's only a few hundred yards away but bullets are slicing by us. I'm hoping the old man and Nya Meh can rouse the defense in time. A bullet grazes Ree Meh's arm, bringing blood, but she doesn't slow down or even flinch.

More yells. More shots. *Let them miss!* I pray.

We enter a patch of thick foliage, where for a minute or two bullets can't get near us. "Go! Run!" I tell her.

"I'm not leaving you here," she says, throwing a quick, desperate glance over her shoulder. It's quiet back there. Too quiet. They must be reloading.

"You have to!"

"No!"

I don't know how to make her go. "The stretcher's slowing us down," I say. "Put him on my back."

Somehow she hoists him up. Dropping everything except my bamboo pole, my canteen, and the rifle, I trot down the trail with the soldier draped across me. I can't risk speeding up to a run—we might fall, and then I'm dead for sure.

With Ree Meh ahead of me, we reach the last set of switchbacks before the river. *Bam!* They're firing again, and she ducks to miss a ricocheting bullet.

"Go get help!" I shout, trying to sound as commanding as Peh. "Now!"

Amazingly it works, because she speeds up and races downhill like a deer.

Now it's just me and this soldier again. The sharp curves in the trail are making it hard for our pursuers to aim, and they don't want to shoot the soldier by mistake. But I'm running out of time before they're right on my heels. The one in the lead is only about four switchbacks behind me now.

186

The trail makes another sharp turn. Just ahead, the river sparkles through the trees. It's wide but shallow, and I spot Ree Meh's small shape sprinting across the near shore. The camp is just across the river. She's almost safe. Where are our defenders? Why aren't they coming?

I could leave the soldier here. He's probably dying anyway, his leg infected and swollen, fever raging through his body. I might make it to camp before they shoot me. I'm a fast runner. I glance at his face. No, I can't drop the boy now. Not here. Not when we've come so far.

I need to buy some time. Lowering his body to the ground, I race back uphill around two switchbacks. At the third bend, I lift the rifle, brace it against my shoulder, and wait. In less than a minute a flash of forest green uniform moves through the leaves, followed by several others. They're not using the trail—they've decided to shoot from the jungle, where they'll be better camouflaged this close to camp.

Before they get too close and realize I'm alone, I start firing. I send off a semicircle of bullets into the leaves. Then I race to the second switchback and shoot off a volley from there. Reaching the place where I've left the boy, I shoot from there, too. I want them to think a dozen Karenni warriors are attacking them.

Then I sling the rifle across my shoulder, pick the boy up in my arms, and stagger down the hill to the river.

13

A dozen or so armed Karenni men come splashing through the water toward me. They pass me without a word, race up the trail, and start shooting into the trees.

I see Ree Meh running toward me as well, and soon she takes the weight of the boy's head and shoulders in her arms. As the water curls around my ankles, I know we've made it. Our attackers will turn and run now. They'd never defy the Thai army by entering a camp on this side of the border.

On the far bank a crowd is gathering around Nya Meh and my mule, Mango, and . . . is that Sa Reh?

Nya Meh wades through the water to us, her eyes on the boy's bleeding, oozing leg.

"Is he alive?"

"Barely."

"Can you carry him a bit farther, to the doctor's hut?" she asks, taking Chiko's swollen leg in her hands.

"We'll use my mule," I say.

We cross the rest of the river together, the three of us using our arms as a makeshift stretcher for the boy.

Sa Reh is clutching the rope around Mango's neck. He's chewing betel nut mix, as usual—his favorite habit, even though I've told him a hundred times that the stuff stains his teeth and makes his breath smell bad.

"Tu Reh!" he says. "Who are these girls? They've been telling us some crazy story that you're carrying a Burmese soldier. . . ." His voice trails off as he sees the boy's uniform. "Is he dead? Did you kill him?"

"Can't talk now," I pant, still trying to catch my breath. I take the rope from Sa Reh, and Mango nuzzles me in welcome. We heave the boy's body across her back.

I hand Sa Reh the rifle. "Give this to the old man, will you?"

People are clustered around the grandfather, listening intently to his story, casting worried looks in our direction. Sa Reh takes the weapon from me, disgust in his face as he backs away from the soldier.

I lead Mango through camp, and Nya Meh and Ree

Meh follow me. Grown-ups murmur and point at the soldier's body. Kids circle around us, poking, pushing, shouting.

"Get back!" Ree Meh orders. Her voice is sharp, and they obey.

It's noon, so most of the kids' mothers are inside, cooking the midday meal. Mua is nowhere in sight. Suddenly I can't wait to see her.

Auntie Doctor is eating, but she leaps to her feet as soon as we enter the medical hut. She doesn't ask any questions about the uniform or the soldier.

"Put him there!" she commands, pointing to an empty cot, rushing to wash her hands. "Who splinted him?"

"I did," Nya Meh answers.

"You—stay with me. The two of you—out!"

We leave the hut, and I take a moment to stroke Mango's muzzle. What a patient creature she is! She's never resisted a load, no matter how heavy. Her coat is clean—looks like Sa Reh or my sister just combed her.

Ree Meh is standing beside me, and I notice her upper arm is bleeding from the bullet that grazed it. "Need a bandage?" I ask.

"I'm fine. I know how to take care of a little cut like this one. I still think I should have stayed with you back there."

"It's okay, Ree Meh. I made it. And besides, you had to get help."

"Grandfather and Nya Meh were doing that already, but it took them a while. You were right about the leaders. Some of them didn't want to let a soldier into camp, but when they found out it was you who was carrying him, they sent the defenders."

"I'm still not sure they'll let him stay," I say, leading Mango forward. "Come on. Let's go home."

But Ree Meh doesn't follow. She stays where she is, and that lost expression comes back for a moment. Suddenly I remember that she doesn't have a home anywhere, not even in camp.

"Tu Reh!"

Finally! Mua and Oo Meh are hurrying toward me as fast as they can.

Mua puts a hand on my arm and looks at me for a long minute. "Is your *peh* all right?"

"As far as I know. Going on with the mission."

Oo Meh is jumping up and down beside me. "Sa Reh took me fishing yesterday," she tells me happily as I tousle her hair. "We caught three big ones, bigger than the one you caught that day—" She stops, catching sight of the girl behind me.

"This is Ree Meh," I say. "Her sister's in the medical hut, helping the doctor. We brought a soldier back with us. A Burmese."

Mua's shoulders stiffen. "I heard. Does your *peh* know you've done this?" she asks.

"Peh wanted me to carry him to safety." He didn't *tell* me to do it, though. And he didn't say anything about bringing the boy to camp. One decision leads to another—that was all he said. Now look at what I've done.

Mua nods slowly. "If your *peh* ordered it, it must be the right thing."

It was my decision, I want to tell her, but I don't. I wonder what I'll have to decide next. Hope it's something easy, like where to sleep tonight so that the girls can stay in our hut.

Mua turns to Ree Meh and smiles warmly. "You come home with me. You can wash up there, and lunch is ready."

"Thank you, Auntie," Ree Meh says. "But I have to check on Grandfather. This was a long journey for him."

"He's inside the president's hut, eating a good meal. I told him I was taking you home with me, and that you'd see him later. Let's take care of that arm first. You're a brave girl."

Ree Meh, my mother, and my sister head for our hut. I follow slowly, one hand clutching Mango's rope and the other curled around my bamboo pole. Oh, for a bath, a meal made by Mua, a mat somewhere, anywhere, for a good long rest. . . .

A strong hand grabs my shoulder and spins me around. "Tu Reh! What's going on?"

It's Sa Reh, of course, gnawing on his betel mix at full

speed. "Nothing," I say, too tired to answer his real question. "I'm heading home."

"It's good to see you back."

"I didn't get to finish the mission," I say.

"Yes, but you caught a spy! Does he have some information about their army's next move? Is he going to tell us what he knows?"

I'm so tired that it's hard to think of anything to say. "We'll have to wait and see. The doctor is working on his leg."

"You can't get information from a dead enemy, right? Are we going to have to *make* him tell the truth, or do you think he'll cooperate?"

"He does what I ask," I manage. It isn't a lie—Chiko tried to convince the grandfather to let him stay, didn't he?

He turns aside to spit out some juice and grins. "It sure looked strange when you came into camp. Seeing you cradling that soldier in your arms like a baby. Who are those girls you brought along, anyway? The older one isn't bad looking, even with that scar on her face."

For some reason this irritates me. "Nya Meh's a healer. She's helping the doctor right now."

"I'd sure like to get to know her better. I'm glad the council's making room for them to stay in camp."

"They are? That's good. Because they don't have anywhere else to go."

"Who does, these days?" Sa Reh claps me on the

shoulder. "You look terrible, Tu Reh. Get some rest. We'll have fun interrogating that soldier together."

I don't have enough energy left to do more than nod, feeling uneasy that I haven't told him the whole truth. The truth is hard for *me* to grasp—I actually abandoned the mission and risked my life to save a Burmese soldier. How will Sa Reh understand the choices I've been making when I don't understand them myself?

I trudge home with Mango, wishing I could dump the weight of my worries onto her back.

14

"Home" in the camp is a bamboo hut on stilts. Looks a bit like our old house in the village, but it's much smaller.

After tying Mango to the stake and making sure she has plenty of water, I'm glad to climb the ladder. I put my bamboo pole where it belongs, against the wall near my sleeping mat. Afternoon sunshine filters through the walls. Sand is piled in one corner of the room, and a pot of rice steams there on a small fire. Mua can make any place on earth feel cozy and peaceful.

The four of us eat quickly. "May I go to the

doctor's to wait for my sister, Auntie?" Ree Meh asks. "She won't know the way here."

"Can you find the medic's hut again on your own?" Mua asks.

"I'll show her!" Oo Meh says eagerly.

"All right, but come right back, my daughter," Mua says. "You have homework to do."

"Do I *have* to go to school tomorrow?" Oo Meh asks.

"Of course. Tu Reh will go also—he's missed enough already." Mua ignores my scowl and gentles her voice. "You should go, too, Ree Meh. Your sister is old enough to stay home, but you need to study."

"I can read and write already, Auntie," Ree Meh answers. "Grandfather taught me."

I guess she's still reluctant to meet the other girls in the camp, and I don't blame her. She'd probably have more fun kickboxing on the field *with* the boys than giggling in the corner *about* the boys.

"Still, you should go," Mua says. "There's so much more to learn in school than reading and writing, and we have an excellent teacher."

Ree Meh nods. It wouldn't be respectful for her to argue any longer with Mua, but I can tell she's not convinced. She starts down the ladder.

I take my sister aside. "Tell her you'll help her meet everybody at school, will you?" I ask. Oo Meh grins and scampers down the ladder.

After they leave, Mua turns to me. "One hour of rest before you do *anything*, Tu Reh. I've never seen you look so tired."

"No, Mua, I'm going now to talk to the camp leaders."

I *am* tired, but I don't want to wait another minute before proving that I'm a patriot. If only Peh were standing with me! There's no question about *his* loyalty to the cause. I picture him trekking through the jungle with the other men, searching for our people in hiding like they're treasure. Would his team run into more soldiers? At least now they have some weapons.

"The leaders know you're resting, Tu Reh," Mua protests. "They told me to send you there later today."

"It's better if I go early. I won't be able to rest until I do." But what am I supposed to say about why I saved a Burmese soldier's life?

I give Mango a pat and head to the building where we gather for meetings. The medic's hut isn't far from here, and I spot Ree Meh and Oo Meh sitting on a flat stone outside it. The doctor and the healer must be fighting hard to save the soldier's leg. If he loses it, he'll need time to recover. I'm just not sure the camp leaders will let him stay that long. I take a deep breath before walking inside the building to face them.

15

The girls' grandfather is sitting with three council members—our president, his top adviser, and Bu Reh, Sa Reh's father, who led the charge across the river to push back the soldiers. Usually the first to fire, Bu Reh manages our stash of weapons and coordinates our defense plans.

Sa Reh's there, too, and he grins a greeting, patting the space on the bench beside him.

I smile back, but stay standing.

"You're early, Tu Reh," the president says. "Did you rest?"

"Mua said you have some questions for me, Uncle."

"The old Karenni says you saved their lives in the jungle when the elephant attacked. Is that right?"

Maybe, but I wouldn't have made it without the loan of the grandfather's rifle. "We watched out for each other," I say.

"Your father always has a good reason for his decisions. Why did he tell you to carry the Burmese boy here?"

"He didn't." I take a deep breath and describe how we heard the mines exploding and found the dead bodies. "Peh bandaged this soldier's leg. Then he had to finish the mission with the other men, so he told me to decide what to do next."

The adviser mutters something to the president that I can't hear. "So *you* decided to take the soldier to the healer's hut?" Bu Reh asks. "And then bring him here?"

I can't help glancing at Sa Reh before replying. "Yes, but—" I stop. How cowardly would it be to pass the blame for that second decision to Ree Meh, the healer, and their grandfather? Besides, I don't want to make it sound like two girls and an old man practically forced me to bring the soldier here. I was alone when I carried the boy down the hill to the river during the last sprint to camp.

"Why *did* you take him to the healer's hut?" asks Bu Reh.

I'm still trying to answer when Sa Reh breaks the silence. "I'll bet you thought we could get some information out of him, Tu Reh."

"I don't think the Burmese boy knows much," the grandfather says quickly. "I questioned him thoroughly once he was able to speak."

"He wasn't conscious when Tu Reh found him," adds Sa Reh, still defending me. "So you couldn't interrogate him then. Right, Tu Reh?"

Bu Reh grunts in disgust. "Didn't matter how much he knew. It wasn't worth saving him. Why didn't you just leave him? Or better yet, kill him?"

Every eye is waiting for my answer. What can I say? That he called for his mother? That his eyelashes reminded me of Oo Meh's? I'm not that brave; I hide behind Sa Reh's suggestion instead. "I thought he might tell us something helpful. We'll have to wait and see."

"And your *peh's* team?" the president asks. "They're one man short now. What about the supplies you were carrying?"

Finally—an easy question. "Peh's strong enough to carry most of my pack along with his, and the others will help. And now they have the dead soldiers' rifles—four of them—and plenty of ammunition." I look right at Bu Reh as I make this announcement.

"I warned Oo Reh to take a rifle or two along," Bu Reh says. "Going on a mission without them is suicide. But he insisted we keep them all. A patriot, no doubt about that, but he has some strange ideas. 'God will defend us,' he told me."

200

I didn't know Peh had turned aside the offer of weapons. He's a council member, too, so the discussion must have happened during one of their meetings. Anyway, I'm gladder than ever that his team now has four good rifles. He's pushing deeper into enemy territory with every passing hour.

"Go get some rest, Tu Reh," the president says. "We'll question your soldier tomorrow, and I want you there."

I don't like the sound of that—"your soldier." Doesn't make me sound patriotic at all. And there's no smile on Sa Reh's face as I leave the building. He glances my way, but I can tell he's confused by my answers. Well, he's not the only one. I'm not sure I handled that interview well at all. *I probably should have listened to Mua and rested first,* I think as I wearily climb the ladder and stretch out on my sleeping mat.

16

It's night before the three girls return, my sister holding tight to Ree Meh's hand.

Nya Meh looks troubled and tired. "Auntie Doctor had to cut it," she says slowly.

"Too bad," says Mua.

I'm surprised by my own frustration. We dragged that soldier all the way here, escaping bullets and an angry elephant, bringing my loyalty into question, and they couldn't save his leg?

Ree Meh untangles her fingers from my sister's grip, picks up the broom, and begins sweeping, even though Mua's just done the job herself and there's not a speck of dust in sight.

Mua takes one look at Ree Meh's face and hands her the piece of cardboard she uses to scoop up dust piles. "Work keeps me from worrying, too," she says gently. "Later I have some embroidery for you to do."

"I can't sew," Ree Meh says, sweeping as though her life depended on it. "Our *mua* taught Nya Meh, but I was too little when she died. I can hunt, though. I killed most of our food in the jungle."

"I'll teach you to sew," Mua says. "In return, will you teach this daughter of mine to shoot? Girls these days need both skills."

Ree Meh smiles and keeps sweeping.

Nya Meh turns to me. "Tu Reh, Auntie Doctor asked for a boy to stay with Chiko through the night—get him water, maybe help him to shift positions. Will you do it?"

"Go, Tu Reh," Mua tells me, rolling up my mat and handing it to me. "You can't stay anyway. It's all girls here for a while."

I really don't want to see that soldier right now. He's made enough trouble for me.

"Please, Tu Reh. The doctor's exhausted, and Chiko asked for you. He trusts you. Won't you stay there just for the night?"

The healer is working her magic again, and I can't bring

203

myself to say no. Well, I need a place to sleep anyway, and the boy will probably be unconscious. "Okay, okay, I'll go."

"We'll join you first thing in the morning," Ree Meh says.

"Good," I say. "The council's going to grill me again, and I need the support."

"I'll come then, too," adds Oo Meh.

"Not you, my daughter," says Mua, making Oo Meh frown. "You have to go to school, remember? Your brother and Ree Meh can meet you there later in the day. I'll send breakfast over, Tu Reh."

I pick up my bamboo pole and start climbing down the ladder, but the healer stops me. "Chiko doesn't know about the leg yet. You'll have to tell him if he wakes up, Tu Reh."

It's a dark night, so nobody spots me heading to the doctor's hut with my sleeping mat tucked under my arm. I don't know what's going to be worse—the interrogation in the morning or having to break the news to the boy about his leg.

17

Auntie Doctor greets me with relief, pulls a curtain around her cot, and starts snoring within minutes.

Leaving the kerosene lantern burning, I spread my mat on the floor near the soldier. I'm not looking forward to telling him about his leg. I've thought a lot about what I would do if it happened to me—so many boys our age are missing legs, arms, fingers, toes. Even eyes. I don't know if I could endure it, but I'd have to, I guess. Just like he will.

He's fast asleep, one hand still stretched across

his pocket. Once again I wonder what's in there. His lashes do look like my sister's—even though I know he's fifteen, he doesn't look much older than ten-year-old Oo Meh. An animal howls somewhere in the jungle, and the boy stirs. His eyes fly open.

"Did they cut it?" he asks right away.

I hesitate. Enemy or no enemy, this is a bad thing to have to tell anybody. "Yes. They had to. They saved your knee, though."

His whole body freezes for a long second, and then he bends one arm across his face.

"I'm . . . I'm sorry," I can't help adding.

He's so still it scares me, so I start talking fast: "They have good replacement legs now. I've seen boys our age playing soccer. Running. Jumping. The fake feet even look like they're real."

I have a feeling I'm making things worse by babbling like this, so I shut up. There's a square of clean bandage on the table; I get it and tuck it into his hand. After a while he presses the cloth against his eyes, even as his other hand travels back to that pocket.

"What's in there?" I ask after a long silence. Partly I'm trying to distract him, but I'm curious, too.

He moves the cloth aside, unbuttons the pocket, takes out two photos, and hands them to me. I stare at them in the flickering light. One is of a Burmese girl. The other is of a young man who looks a bit familiar.

"This is your brother?" I ask, forgetting to speak Burmese for a second.

"My *peh*." He uses the Karenni word; he must have overheard us using it.

"You look a lot like him."

He lifts his head to see my face. "Really? How?"

I take a moment to study the photo again. Their features aren't the same, really. So why is there such a strong resemblance? "You have the same look in your eyes. It's like . . . like maybe you're thinking about the same kinds of things. Where is he?"

"In prison. For resisting the government."

"How long has he been there?"

"Eight months. I'd do anything to get him out of prison. Anything. But now what can I do, with my leg missing?" He flops back on the bed again and winces in pain.

I don't know how to answer his question. "How did you end up as a soldier?"

"They grabbed me and forced me into it. I wanted to be a teacher, not a soldier." His voice breaks, and he fumbles for the cloth again and presses it against his eyes.

For some reason I want to keep distracting him. I hold up the other photo in the flickering light. "And this girl?"

"My neighbor." His voice is flat, but he peers out from under the cloth.

"Must be a special neighbor for you to carry her around in your pocket all this time." I hand the photos back.

"She is. She was." He tucks the photos into his pocket and refastens the button.

"Are you in pain?"

"No. But I'm sleepy."

"The doctor must have given you painkillers. I'm staying here tonight. Wake me if you need anything."

"Thank you. I'm glad you'll be here."

It's my turn to take something out of a pocket. "Here are your glasses. Third time now?"

He takes them from me, and I catch a trace of a smile. Once again I'm reminded of Oo Meh. This boy can't be a spy. He's not even much of a soldier.

"Tomorrow the camp leaders are coming to ask you questions," I say suddenly. "Tell them what you told me about your father being in prison and how they forced you into the army. Your life depends on convincing them that you're not a spy. Can you do it, Chiko?"

There's a rustling outside the open window. I hurry to the window and glimpse a shadow disappearing into the bamboo. It looks familiar, and my heart sinks. How long was Sa Reh standing there? How much did he overhear?

"Who was that?" Chiko asks.

"Nobody. Get some sleep."

18

I'm so tired that not even the thought of Sa Reh overhearing me talking to Chiko can keep me awake. I don't stir until I hear Nya Meh and Ree Meh arriving early the next morning. Before they enter the room, I hurry out the back door to splash water on my face and comb my hair with my fingers.

When I come back Nya Meh is helping the doctor clean Chiko's wound and rebandage his stump.

"It looks better," Auntie Doctor says. "As soon as it's healed we can get it fitted for a prosthetic.

Nya Meh, I'd like to teach you how to do this kind of surgery. It can save lives if you do it right."

"I'd like to learn, Auntie Doctor," she says.

Ree Meh serves me the breakfast Mua sent along. "I am saying a prayer for quick healing, my brother," she tells Chiko as she puts a plate of rice by his cot.

Chiko doesn't answer; he's gritting his teeth as the wound is cleaned. Auntie Doctor gives him an injection, and he manages to eat once the pain has diminished.

"Is he going to be ready when they question him?" Ree Meh asks her sister.

"I hope so," Nya Meh says.

It isn't long before the girls' grandfather and the three council members enter the room, with Sa Reh at his father's heels. I brace myself for this second round. I know they're coming to question Chiko, but somehow I feel like it's me who's on trial.

The four men stand in a semicircle beside the cot, with Sa Reh behind them. The doctor is at the foot of the cot; Nya Meh, Ree Meh, and I are behind her. This means that Chiko's surrounded by Karenni faces, and he shifts uncomfortably as his eyes dart around the room.

"Tell us about your mission," the president asks him in Burmese.

For long moment Chiko gazes at the healer, as though he's drawing the strength he needs from her calm expression. Sa Reh frowns as he catches this unspoken communication between a Burmese soldier and a Karenni girl.

"Speak up, boy!" orders Bu Reh.

"Our captain didn't like me much," Chiko says. "He ordered me to walk ahead and make sure the way was clear for the others. I didn't do my job. One of my friends was killed—he was a good boy."

"Did you have a weapon?"

"No. The captain didn't trust me with a rifle."

"That's a lie!" It's Sa Reh, sticking to Karenni. "Tu Reh had a rifle when he came into camp."

"That one was mine," says the grandfather quickly. "I gave it to Tu Reh. And he used it just as a Karenni man should."

"I'm not good with a rifle," Chiko says. "I was the mine clearer—that was my job. I could never kill anybody, I promise."

"He's lying, I tell you! His father's a criminal!" It's Sa Reh again.

"What? How do you know this?" the president asks, turning to face Sa Reh.

"I heard him last night. He said he'd do anything to get his father out of jail. Ask him."

"Is it true your father's a criminal?" the president asks in Burmese.

Chiko looks at me. Slowly he takes the photo of his father from his pocket. "My *peh* is in prison for resisting the government." Again he uses the Karenni word for father, a smart move, but his Burmese then grows so proper I can barely understand him. "He is the one who first told me about your courageous fight for freedom. He had a beloved Karenni friend when he was in university."

The photo passes from hand to hand until it reaches the grandfather.

"You look like him," the old man says.

"That's what Tu Reh said, too," says Chiko.

Did he *have* to share that? It makes us sound like we're friends.

Suddenly Sa Reh snatches the photo from the old man's hand and flings it on the floor. "He's an enemy! A Burmese! Why are we treating him as a guest?"

"Be still!" It's Bu Reh. The look he gives his son could make a troop of soldiers put down their rifles.

Sa Reh takes a step back, eyes on the ground. His mouth is still; he's stopped chewing for once.

I feel a twinge for my friend. I'd be ashamed, too, if my *peh* corrected me like that. But Peh would be just as furious as Sa Reh's father if I was the one to disrespect an old man like that.

Nya Meh picks up the photo and hands it to Chiko.

"Thank you, my sister," Chiko says, and she smiles.

The president doesn't like this friendliness between a Karenni girl and a Burmese boy any more than Sa Reh did. "Step back, girl," he tells Nya Meh sharply. "Your training center, soldier. Where is it? How big? And who runs it?"

Chiko obeys with a lengthy description. My Burmese is decent, but I'm finding it hard to keep up. He's still using a lot of big words I've never heard.

"I know that place," Auntie Doctor says suddenly. "Used to be a Karenni school, I think. There's a gym, and it's near the river, right?"

"That's where new recruits sleep," Chiko replies. "Have you been there?"

"Yours isn't the first Burmese leg I've amputated, young man. A couple of soldiers I treated in the clinic also told me about that school."

"I'm glad to hear your words, Doctor," the grandfather says suddenly. "Listening to this interrogation, I was beginning to wonder if Karenni ways of hospitality have changed faster than I realized. In my day, we knew how to treat an enemy. It's in the Book, isn't it? Please excuse me. I'll be waiting in the church if you need me."

It's the president's turn to seem a bit ashamed. The grandfather pats Sa Reh on the shoulder as he leaves.

The questioning continues. Chiko describes the training regimen, estimates the number of soldiers and recruits who pass through the center, and shares a few details from letters that came from army headquarters. After a while, though, Chiko starts to sweat, and soon he's clenching his jaw in pain.

Nya Meh reaches to straighten the sheet over Chiko's leg and gives the doctor a quick look.

"Our patient is suffering," Auntie Doctor says immediately. "He needs more medicine."

"That's enough for now. We'll decide what to do with him at our next council meeting. Thank you, Doctor." The president turns to the girls with a smile, obviously trying to make amends for the crisp tone he used earlier with Nya Meh. "We're glad you're safe with us now, my daughters. I hear one of you is quite a healer."

"I try, Uncle," Nya Meh says. "I'd like to train to be a real doctor someday."

Auntie Doctor is trying to herd as many people as she can out of the room. "She definitely has the gift. I'd be happy to teach her. Now if you'd kindly step outside, Nya Meh and I can give this boy his medicine."

"Your *peh* was a brave man," Bu Reh tells Ree Meh as we walk to the threshold. "I fought beside him once or twice."

Ree Meh smiles for the first time. "Thank you, Uncle."

The men start walking to the council headquarters, and Sa Reh follows without saying a word to me. "Maybe I should go with them," I say.

"But your *mua* said you had to go to school, Tu Reh," Ree Meh reminds me.

"School! Hah!" I snort, but I stay where I am. "My *peh* thought I was ready to skip it—he took me on the mission, didn't he?"

214

Ree Meh sighs. "I know. Come on—maybe I can talk Nya Meh into joining us."

Girls. What a mystery. This one stayed beside me in the jungle with bullets flying around her head. Now she doesn't want to face a dozen or so girls her age.

19

Inside, Auntie Doctor is sitting and mopping her face. "I'm getting too old for this kind of pressure. Give the boy his painkillers, will you, Nya Meh?"

But Chiko props himself up on his elbow, his glasses askew. "If I could get back to the training camp, the army might send me back to Yangon. I'm not much use as a soldier now."

"You need to heal from your surgery before you do anything," Auntie Doctor says, and then she switches to Karenni so he can't understand. "I hope the council decides to let him stay until that happens."

"What are they going to do? Send him back into

the jungle like this?" Ree Meh asks. She's using our language, too. Nobody wants to dim the hope in Chiko's face. Not even me.

"The president didn't seem too convinced that he wasn't a spy," I say. "And now he's seen our leaders and our camp firsthand. I hope they take it to a vote."

"What if they do the right thing and let him stay?" Nya Meh asks quietly, handing Chiko a glass of water and three pills. It's an effort for him to swallow them.

Auntie Doctor considers this option for a minute. "He might have a chance to get home if that happens," she says finally. "Once he's strong enough, we'd have to figure out a way to transport him to the clinic where we make replacement legs. His training camp really isn't too far from there—a long walk uphill and down again on a good road. In fact, I'll be heading to the clinic in a week or so. If he heals quickly and they let him come along, I could clear him at the checkpoint. Those Thai soldiers owe me a favor or two."

It takes half a day to get to the clinic. The doctor walks it, but how would Chiko make it there with only one leg? Suddenly an outrageous idea leaps into my head. It sounds so much like something Peh would suggest that I wonder for a second if he's in the room. He's in my brain, that's for sure. *No, Peh,* I tell him silently. *I can't do that. I won't.*

Chiko is almost asleep now, lulled by the medicine

and the sound of low voices in a conversation he can't understand. He's shivering, though. "Maybe we could carry him there on a stretcher, like we did before," Nya Meh says, covering him with a blanket.

"Tu Reh and I could do it," Ree Meh offers. "We brought him here like that almost all the way. We can do it again."

"No, my daughter," the doctor says wearily. "It's not safe for you, even if we could get a clearance. The men leave me alone because I'm old and I've treated so many of them—Burmese, Thai, Karenni. They're starting to seem the same to me. Boys, all of them. Boys in pain."

A wave of anger takes my breath away. How dare she say that we Karenni boys are like the Burmese? I'd never storm into a peaceful village to fling a torch on somebody's roof. But I watched a Burmese soldier do that to my house, and then heard him laugh as I ran.

"The camp won't let him stay," I say. "They'll probably make *me* carry him back to the jungle, where I should have left him in the first place."

Nya Meh's voice is gentle. "Don't look back now," she says. "You did the right thing."

"He'd be dead if you hadn't brought him here," Auntie Doctor adds. "The infection was bad, and spreading fast. Now he needs to sleep long and hard, and in the meantime I want to teach Nya Meh a bit more about the surgery. You two—off to school."

218

My fists are still clenched, and I don't budge. How did I end up in this mess?

"Won't you go with me, sister?" Ree Meh asks. She hasn't moved either, and I can hear the anxiety in her voice. "Please?"

"I want to spend as much time as I can learning from Auntie Doctor before she leaves," says Nya Meh. "Grandfather wants you to go, Ree Meh. He told me that I didn't have to."

Somehow, mysteriously, Ree Meh's worry over school has extinguished my anger like a bucket of water. "You'll be just fine," I tell her. "My sister and I will be there, remember?"

"Maybe *I* should have stayed in the jungle," she says glumly.

20

Ree Meh and I walk out together, leaving the doctor and Nya Meh consulting in quiet voices over a thick medical book. "School's that way," I say, pointing down the path with my pole. Standing tensely on the threshold, she reminds me of a hunted deer.

"Your *mua* actually said we had to go after lunch, remember? She'd like it if you gave me a tour of the camp first, Tu Reh, wouldn't she?"

Her smile is sudden and sweet. Besides, Mua is always scolding me to be more pleasant, and offering a tour of the camp would be hospitable, right?

We stroll side by side down the path. The sun is

climbing high behind the mountains, and bamboo leaves on both banks shake lightly in the breeze. A bridge spans the deepest, widest part of the river. It's a good place to fish. We pass the building that's used for meetings and a smaller one that serves as our school. The two buildings face each other across an open field where a group of kids are kicking a soccer ball, laughing and joking. Just as I told Chiko, two boys are playing with replacement legs.

Barbed wire borders the camp on one side; the river, edged with bamboo, marks the other side. We've built several rickety wooden watchtowers to keep an eye out for invaders. The dense jungle, the threat of attack, and hidden mines keep us away from the Burmese side. An army checkpoint and the threat of arrest block any escape on the Thai side.

The gate in the wire fence is open, and there's no guard posted there. "Is it always open, Tu Reh?" Ree Meh asks, studying the dirt road that leads away from the entrance.

I nod, remembering the hopes I'd had of escaping into Thailand when we'd first arrived. I talked with Peh of blending in, trying to make a living, saving money to buy some land and plant rice. It didn't take long to find out how impossible that would be. "Thai soldiers have a checkpoint just around the bend," I tell her. "If a Karenni is caught anywhere outside the camp without clearance, he's arrested and handed to the Burmese police."

Leaning on my pole, I watch the cool, silver river twisting through the valley. It's the same river that passes through our village. We walked along it to get here. It comes all the way through the jungle, linking us back to the place where I first waded, fished, and learned to swim.

"Look at all that bamboo," Ree Meh says.

"You should have seen our grove at home,right next to the rice paddies." I say. "We're not supposed to plant rice here, you know."

"But we ate rice for breakfast. And dinner. Where does your *mua* get it?"

"Supplies come twice a month," I answer. "An American brings rice, oil, dried milk, sugar, soybeans, charcoal—things like that. Another man, a missionary from Europe, brings kerosene, medical supplies, and shoes."

"Generous people," Ree Meh says.

I shrug. "We Karenni have always made our own way. Now we owe our lives to these foreigners."

"My sister would say we owe our lives to God," says Ree Meh.

"Even after what they did to her?" I ask.

There's a loud exclamation of disgust behind us, and we spin around. Sa Reh is standing there. For a wild second, hope rises inside me—maybe he's finally giving me the benefit of the doubt. But when our eyes meet, his are burning like coals.

He turns to Ree Meh, teeth grinding the betel mix tucked in his cheek. "What did they do to your sister?"

"I'm not sure," Ree Meh answers. "I can only guess."

"Tell me what you know!" he commands.

I can tell Ree Meh's getting angry. "Ask her yourself if you're so curious!" she flings back.

"I don't need to." He takes a step closer to me, and I smell the mix of nuts, tobacco, coconut, green leaves, and limestone paste on his breath. "I can't believe you'd actually bring a Burmese soldier to a girl who went through something like that. Didn't you think about the memories she must have about that uniform?"

"I did," I say. "But—"

Sa Reh interrupts. "No excuses. How could you do it? How could you take that soldier to her? Risking your life and theirs—for his?"

"Our lives were already in danger," Ree Meh says. "They were coming for us, didn't you hear that?"

"He could have left the soldier and brought you here to safety."

"That 'soldier' is just a boy! He's younger than you are, if you hadn't noticed."

Ree Meh and Sa Reh are shouting at each other while I'm standing there doing nothing, saying nothing.

"He's an enemy!" Sa Reh bellows.

"He would have died if we'd left him there!" Ree Meh yells.

223

Now Sa Reh's eyes are on me. "That scum should have died," he says, and walks away.

Before Ree Meh and I have a chance to talk, Oo Meh comes running up. "Mua wants you both home for lunch. And then it's time for school." She looks over her shoulder at Sa Reh's retreating figure. "Why was *he* so mad?"

"I don't know," I answer.

But I do know.

Thanks to my decisions in the jungle, I've lost my best friend in camp, probably forever.

21

Mua tells us the council has chosen a site for the girls and their grandfather. It's close to the river, a bit away from the other huts.

"Unmarried girls need privacy, so it's good that it's set apart," she says, serving us dried fish and rice. "Tu Reh, you must help them build it. After school, of course. And you'll have to find somewhere else to sleep until it's ready."

"Yes, Mua," I answer. Hard work will take my mind off my worries, and besides, I don't mind spending every minute I can with . . . working.

Building the hut, of course. Making it secure for the girls and their grandfather.

After lunch my sister, Ree Meh, and I walk to school. "I told the other girls about you this morning," Oo Meh says, clutching Ree Meh's hand. "They can't believe how brave you were, living in the jungle with just your sister and your grandfather. I told them how you used to hunt your own food, and they want to hear all about it."

Ree Meh looks slightly less anxious, and I ruffle my sister's hair. When did she get so smart?

The teacher enrolls Ree Meh with a welcoming smile. Like Chiko, he stepped on a mine when he was a boy. Now he bounds around the classroom on his prosthetic, telling jokes and waving his hands in the air as he teaches history, math, ethics, science. If he weren't so interesting, I might put up more resistance to my parents' school-until-you're-eighteen rule, but he's one of the best teachers around.

Thanks to Oo Meh's buildup, the other girls greet Ree Meh warmly. They come up to her at recess as if she's a magnet. I watch her standing with her chin up, fielding questions about life in the jungle, and admire how she hides her nervousness.

Meanwhile, some of the boys gather around me.

"Did you really save that Burmese boy's life, Tu Reh?"

I nod.

Someone snickers. "Gotten soft, haven't you?"

"What does Sa Reh think?" another boy asks.

I shrug and walk away. Sa Reh is easily the best kick-boxer in camp, tells the funniest jokes, and once single-handedly killed a king cobra that slithered into church. Younger kids especially look up to him—he takes them fishing and plays games with them for hours when the rest of us won't. When Sa Reh made me his best friend, this strange new place felt a bit like home. Now what am I going to do?

Thankfully, work on the girls' new home gets under way that afternoon, and it's a distraction. Nya Meh is still in the doctor's hut, but Ree Meh and I start cutting bamboo. We use Mango to haul the heavy loads. The grandfather sits on the bank, weaving smaller bamboo strips into a lattice for the windows and door.

"We work together well," I tell Ree Meh quietly, so the old man can't hear.

She smiles, moving her braid over her shoulder to keep it out of the way.

Oo Meh stops by to "help." "The council decided to let the whole camp vote on Chiko," she informs us.

"How did you find out?" Ree Meh asks.

"This one knows it's going to storm before the clouds do," I say. I'm relieved because the news means that the council wasn't unanimous about taking Chiko back to the jungle right away.

I can't ruffle Oo Meh's wispy hair like I usually do when I tease her because she's somehow managed to weave it into a thin, scraggly braid. She tosses it around every five minutes and stays glued to our side, chatting constantly and focusing on Ree Meh's every move. I can't blame my sister. I'm having trouble controlling my own eyes.

When it gets too dark to work, the old man heads to the place where he's staying, and the three of us go back to my hut.

Nya Meh's already there. "How is he?" Ree Meh asks her sister.

"On the outside, healing well. But on the inside? Sad. Quiet. The doctor asked for you to stay there tonight, Tu Reh. And so did Chiko."

Not again! Well, what do I have to lose? Besides, my mat is still there and I don't really have any other place to sleep.

This time Chiko's awake when I get there.

"Feeling better?" I ask.

"A bit. Not much to do except think about this, though." He gestures to where his leg used to be. "Where were you all day?"

"At school. My parents are making me go until I'm eighteen. My friend—a boy I know—stopped when he was fourteen. He spends time with the men while I'm stuck doing lessons with a bunch of children."

"I'd love to study something—something hard to take my mind off this. You learn in Karenni, right?"

"Right. Teacher tries to teach us English, but we're hopeless at it."

"My *peh* taught me English. I can read and write it, too."

I yawn and spread out my sleeping mat. "Maybe we've got some English books in the schoolroom."

His eyes get wide behind his glasses. "Books? Really? I haven't read a book in months. *Months,* Tu Reh!"

"I'll ask tomorrow. Go to sleep now, Chiko."

But he's not done yet. "Your teacher any good?"

"He's not bad. In fact, you should meet him. He stepped on a mine years ago. Lost his knee, too, but he can still chase and catch the little ones just fine."

"Really?"

"Really. Now go to sleep."

"One more thing." He hesitates. "What's going to happen to me, Tu Reh? Do your leaders think I'm a spy?"

"I'm not sure," I say. "The council called a camp vote for this Friday. They'll decide what to do with you then."

"Will they—will they kill me?"

"No. I don't know what they'll do, but they won't murder you." *They might make me carry you back to the jungle and leave you there,* I think, but I don't say it out loud.

He sighs in relief and settles down to sleep. I shake my head as I stretch out on my mat. This boy believes everything I tell him. For his sake, I hope I'm right.

22

In the morning my first thought is of Peh, searching for Karenni in the jungle. It's been a week since we said good-bye. What dangers is he facing? Will he, too, come back without a leg, an arm, his eyes? Will he come back at all?

Chiko's still asleep when Ree Meh and the healer arrive, bringing breakfast again from Mua. "I want to teach you about antibiotics today, Nya Meh," Auntie Doctor says. "They are miracle medicines, but you have to use them sparingly."

Ree Meh and I head off to school. "Ready for your second day?" I ask.

"It's not as bad as I thought it would be," she admits. "Thanks to your sister, the girls think I'm some kind of hero."

"You are," I say, and she smiles.

We part ways at the door, and she makes her way to the girls' side of the room. At recess, when the other boys surround me again, I ignore their questions and teasing and walk away. I'm almost as good at kickboxing as Sa Reh, and the strongest wrestler in school by far, so they don't follow me.

Before I leave that afternoon, I quietly approach the teacher. I know I can trust him. He used to scold Sa Reh and me about the way we hated the Burmese. "Revenge makes you a prisoner," he'd tell us, and we'd nod, but afterward we'd joke about how he probably lost his manhood along with his leg.

"I do have a few English books that a foreigner left behind," the teacher says now. "Why do you want them?"

"They're for the Burmese boy in the doctor's hut," I say, keeping my voice low. "He can read English. And he misses books."

"I'll take them to him myself," the teacher says. "Your soldier sounds like a smart kid, Tu Reh."

There it is again—"my" soldier. Am I ever going to change that?

That afternoon Nya Meh comes to visit the site for the new hut. She's carrying an empty bucket. "The doctor needs more water," she tells us.

Ree Meh describes for her sister how we're going to orient the building, with the windows facing the river and the door toward the village.

Smiling her approval, Nya Meh wades into the shallows to fill the bucket. Ree Meh, Mango, and I are heading to the far shore to cut more bamboo when we hear splashing behind us. I turn to see Sa Reh approaching the healer. He's ignoring me and Ree Meh completely, but for once he's not chewing betel nut.

"I did tell him to talk to her," Ree Meh mutters. "But I didn't think he'd take me up on it."

I try not to make it seem like I'm staring or spying. Sa Reh's interest in the healer seems curious to me, but maybe he just wants to get to know her better. He did say he thought she was pretty.

I see him take Nya Meh's bucket. After filling it for her, he stands beside her for a while. I can't hear them, but I can tell he's doing most of the talking, with Nya Meh listening intently.

Let her talk, too, I want to tell him. But who am I to give advice? Some kind of girl expert? It's a good thing Ree Meh likes to work without talking because I'm not too confident about my own conversation skills.

As Sa Reh and Nya Meh leave the river together, I can't help feeling a bit more hopeful. If anybody can convince Sa Reh that I did the right thing, it's Nya Meh. Maybe they'll get to that subject soon.

Ree Meh, her grandfather, and I work on the girls' hut until dinnertime. Nya Meh joins us later that evening. She doesn't say anything about Sa Reh, and her sister doesn't ask. Neither do I, of course, but I can't help wanting to know what they talked about. Did he tell her more than he told me about losing his mother? He changed the subject when I brought it up once or twice after he confided in me. But I still have my *mua*, and neither Nya Meh nor Sa Reh have theirs.

I'm glad to see that the girls' company keeps Mua from worrying too much about Peh. When we give thanks for the meal, she says a prayer for Peh's safety, and her voice trembles. But afterward, beside the fire, mending clothes and talking, she seems to forget her fears as she tells the girls stories from her childhood. I stay as long as I can, enjoying their teasing and laughter, but soon Mua shoos me out the door.

After the lively talk inside our hut, the long walk to the doctor's hut seems dark and dull. Chiko will be waiting for me there, with his stump, his sad eyes, and his questions. Suddenly I long for Sa Reh's company. I wish he could be there with me—to banter insults back and forth, and maybe even to make Chiko laugh.

As I pass Sa Reh's hut, on an impulse I climb halfway up the ladder and peek inside like I used to before I left for the mission. A few men are gathered around a map, pointing and talking. Sa Reh spots me first and—I can't believe he does this—actually spits a gob of red betel juice right at me. It lands short, but the men look up, and I see that they're Bu Reh's allies—the toughest warriors in camp.

"Looking for a new place to sleep, Tu Reh?" asks Bu Reh. His tone is pleasant, but I notice he hasn't scolded his son for spitting at me. "Why not come all the way up?"

I don't move. "No. No, thanks. I'm all right."

"Can't wait for the meeting on Friday," he says, sitting back in his chair. "We've got a plan for your soldier that we think the camp is going to like."

The men laugh. "*He* won't like it," Sa Reh says, tipping his head in my direction.

"Isn't that Oo Reh's boy?" one of Bu Reh's cronies asks. "How did a brave man like that let his own son get soft?"

Bu Reh shrugs. "I'm looking forward to asking him when he gets back."

I make myself climb down the ladder before I leap into the room and kick someone—preferably Sa Reh.

I'm *not* soft! I care just as much about the cause as they do! Thankfully, their reminder of Peh brings to mind that surprising moment when he put his hands on my shoulders and looked me in the eye. *He* knows what kind of Karenni man I am, at least—and that's what counts. My thoughts turn to the plan they're concocting. It can't be good news for Chiko, I'm sure.

When I get to the hut, Chiko is holding a book close to his face in the dim light of the kerosene lantern.

"Your teacher came by," he tells me. "He told me all about getting a new leg. He walks decently, Tu Reh."

"Told you."

"If he can be a teacher with only one leg, why can't I?"

"You probably could if you wanted to."

"He loaned me three books in English—they're called *The Lord of the Rings*. Written by a British author. He hasn't read them, but the foreigner who gave them to him told him they were good. I'm almost halfway done with the first one. It *is* good, Tu Reh. Want me to read you a bit? I can try to translate it into Burmese."

"Not now. We need to sleep. Tomorrow you can finish it."

"But Frodo has the Ring, Tu Reh. The Ring!" He hands me the book and his glasses reluctantly.

I have no idea what he's talking about. I put his things on the nightstand beside his bed, make sure he has water to drink, and blow out the lamp.

23

The next afternoon, I spot Sa Reh and the healer sitting on the bridge where he and I used to fish. Again he's talking earnestly, and the healer's listening, her eyes fixed on his face. Nya Meh smiles as I pass, but Sa Reh ignores me.

Sa Reh's not the only one in camp who wants nothing to do with me. The teasing at school is getting worse each day. Adults are brushing past me, too, not meeting my eyes—not many, but enough to make me wish Peh were here to stand with me on Friday. This council meeting is my last chance to prove that

I'm still a Karenni fighter. I have to show them all that I'm the same Tu Reh I was before I left on the mission.

But am I? That night, as Chiko talks about his home, family, and dreams for the future, I can hardly believe this is me, Tu Reh, listening to a Burmese soldier. Am I forgetting? I close my eyes to picture the soldiers who threw the burning torch on our house and bamboo grove. Sadness comes winging back like an arrow. I'd still do anything to get our village back—anything to keep my people alive. But somehow this boy isn't a part of that anymore.

"Your *mua* came by to bring me lunch," Chiko tells me. "She reminds me a lot of my mother."

I'm glad Mua came. She never questioned me after hearing what Peh said, but I could tell that she had doubts. Now that she's met Chiko, I'm sure she understands exactly why I decided to bring him here. "Her Burmese isn't great," I say. "Were you able to talk?"

"She asked a lot of questions about my family. And she told me about your home in the village, Tu Reh. And how it was burned. I'm—I'm sorry."

I can't answer. It's a strange sensation, hearing a Burmese soldier apologize. What am I supposed to say?

"Do you have dreams for the future, Tu Reh?" Chiko asks suddenly.

"Not as big as yours," I say. "Some land, some rice, a family, a home. That's all."

"That's enough. Who needs more than that? I hope you get it."

"I hope so, too."

His leg is healing well, but his face grows sad as he reaches out to finger the bandages on the stump. It's gone forever—there's no changing that. But will he survive long enough to get a replacement? Or will the camp decide that he's too much of a risk?

When Friday comes I can hardly concentrate on school. Ree Meh and I work on the hut through the afternoon without saying much. Tonight's the meeting. Tonight the people will decide what to do with Chiko. Somehow I'm going to have to prove to Sa Reh and everybody else in camp that I'm my father's son, a patriot, a man for the Karenni. I keep slashing and cutting bamboo for a while even after Ree Meh leaves to get ready. The familiar motion relaxes my tense muscles.

When I arrive at the meeting, the large room is already packed. Auntie Doctor is sitting with Mua and the girls in the second row. The president gestures to me, and I join the grandfather on the bench in front of the girls. Sa Reh and his father are across the aisle. Sa Reh's face is stony, and he doesn't glance my way.

I'm not on trial. I haven't done anything wrong. So why does it feel like I'm about to get sentenced? *Peh, where are you?* Wouldn't it be amazing if he got back right now, right this minute? But I know his mission isn't finished. Peh would never come back early if he could help it.

As usual, the pastor starts the meeting with a prayer and a Bible reading before the president takes over.

"Come up here, Tu Reh."

I rise and go forward. "Tell the people how and why you brought your soldier to the healer's hut."

Trying not to flinch at his choice of words, I keep my eyes on Ree Meh as I tell the whole story again, sticking to the facts. The room is quiet as people listen closely.

"And then Peh told me I had to choose what to do. So I decided to take the soldier to the healer's hut."

"Why?" the president asks, but he doesn't sound accusing. Not yet, anyway.

I take a deep breath. "He's younger than I am," I say. "I couldn't leave him there to be killed by animals."

"Why didn't you do a mercy killing, then?" The question rings out from the back of the room; I can't tell who's asking it.

I shrug. "He's just a boy," I say again. "Go and see for yourself. He's in the doctor's hut."

"He's a spy! His father's a criminal!" This time I know who said the words—they came from the front row. From Sa Reh's angry mouth.

"Raise your hands to comment, please," the president says. "We must have order in our meetings. And Tu Reh's right. The soldier is quite young. I questioned him myself, and I personally don't believe he's a spy. Others might still have doubts, but I'm fairly sure this particular soldier doesn't know much."

My heart lifts. Somehow Chiko managed to convince the right person that he was telling the truth. Those big words he used must have helped.

"Thank you, Tu Reh," the president continues. "We don't forget what your *peh*'s doing right now for our people. And that you're his son. Be seated."

I slide back onto the bench, relieved. Maybe I'm finally done with this whole mess. But across the way, Sa Reh is still glowering. And in front Bu Reh is muttering something to the man sitting beside him.

"The next question, then, is what to do with the soldier now that he's here," says the president. "Any suggestions?"

24

Bu Reh raises his hand and gets permission to speak. "Once he's able to leave the medic's hut, he'll find out more about us and our plans. Spy or no spy, we have to get rid of him now."

"Yes, but how?" the president asks.

"Kill him!" That same voice rings from the back of the church. "He's Burmese!"

A few people cheer here and there.

The grandfather stands up suddenly. He's a small man, but suddenly the room grows quiet. "May I speak, sir?" he asks the president.

The president nods.

Slowly the old man turns to face the crowd. "As you've heard already, this soldier is a boy, forced into the army against his will. Now he's suffered the loss of his leg. Doesn't God command us to defend *all* who are weak, my dear friends, not just those who speak our Karenni language? We must think carefully about how we treat this young stranger. If we give way to hatred, we won't be any better than our enemies. I could no longer call myself a Karenni if we killed him."

This is what Peh was trying to tell me in the jungle, I realize. It's what we need to hear again and again, each time we're attacked, oppressed, beaten down. Suddenly I can't stop myself. "They can't control us!" I call out, leaping to my feet. "We are the Karenni!"

And then I know exactly what to do. Saluting the flag in the front of the room, I start singing the national anthem. My voice is terrible, but it's loud, and Ree Meh and Mua join in by the third word. The pastor grabs his guitar to strum an accompaniment. Soon all of us—the president, Bu Reh, and even Sa Reh—are standing, saluting, and singing our Karenni song in unison.

When we're done, the room explodes in loud cheers. The president has to rap the table several times before people start to sit down.

He waits until it's quiet. "Thank you for reminding us of how we must live, my father," he says to the old man.

"But the question remains, my fellow Karenni. What shall we do with our stranger?"

I can hardly believe it. Like magic, the pronoun has changed—Chiko isn't just mine anymore. And the word *soldier* has turned into *stranger*.

But Bu Reh raises his hand. "We've been studying the maps. There's a path not too deep into the jungle that the Burmese have been taking lately. A couple of men can carry him there—my son and I will go along as defenders. We could leave the soldier and come back within a couple of hours."

"Not a bad idea, Bu Reh—" the president begins.

"Are you crazy?" It's Auntie Doctor. "That boy will die in the jungle on his own. The Burmese might never find him. Animals will tear him to shreds. It's just the same as killing him."

"What do you suggest, then, Doctor?" Bu Reh asks.

Auntie Doctor strides forward. "I'll leave in the morning. The boy can come with me. He'll be fitted with a replacement leg at the clinic in the next camp and walk across the border himself."

The president shrugs. "That's impossible, Doctor. You can't carry the boy, and you're the only one with clearance to leave our camp. We'll have to go with Bu Reh's plan."

Someone taps me on the shoulder. Ree Meh, Nya Meh, Mua, and my sister are behind me. Nya Meh gives me a pleading look. Ree Meh is clasping Mua's hand, but her eyes hold mine for a long second. And my sister? It's late for her, way past her bedtime, so she's fighting to stay awake. Her lashes are long on her cheeks as she blinks hard.

Suddenly my hand shoots into the air. *One decision leads to another, right, Peh?*

"Yes, Tu Reh?"

I stand again. "The doctor can borrow my mule, sir," I say.

Sa Reh leaps to his feet. "*What?* That's the only mule in camp!"

The president looks doubtful. "She does belong to you, Tu Reh. But do you really want to do this?"

"Auntie Doctor can bring her back the next time she returns to our camp," I reply.

"What would your *peh* say? And have you cleared this with your *mua?*"

Mua rises slowly, with dignity. "We trust our son's decisions," she announces, her voice clear and strong. "Tu Reh's a smart boy, just like his *peh.*"

The grandfather's old hand is warm on my shoulder. "A man for the Karenni!" he says in my ear.

The vote for the doctor's plan to transport Chiko to the clinic is almost unanimous, except for my former best friend and a few disgruntled faces here and there.

A man for the Karenni! As the meeting adjourns, Peh's voice in my head repeats the old man's words, making it easier to endure Sa Reh ignoring me as he strides out the door. I catch sight of Nya Meh slipping out to follow him.

Auntie Doctor comes over to clasp my hand. "I'll need to attend to a patient or two tonight. Go to Chiko quickly, Tu Reh. We don't want to keep him in suspense. And I'd like to get an early start in the morning. The sooner we get him out of here, the better."

I walk Mua, Ree Meh, and my sister to the hut. Nya Meh is perched on the bottom rung of the ladder to our house. Sa Reh is standing beside her, but as soon as he spots us he disappears into the darkness.

Mango is there, and I stroke her soft muzzle. I'm going to miss her, but I'm trusting that she'll come back when it's time for Auntie Doctor to visit our camp again. "Is he still mad?" I ask the healer.

"It's going to take time," Nya Meh answers.

"We'll all have to get up early to send the doctor and the boy on their way," Mua says as she starts to climb the ladder. "Tu Reh, go tell that poor boy the news."

But I don't leave right away because Ree Meh is lingering at the foot of the ladder. "Did you know you were going to offer your mule, Tu Reh?" she asks.

"No. I thought about it once before, but . . . well, I'm glad I said something now."

"I thought of it, too, but Nya Meh told me to shut up and not say anything. 'He needs to think of this himself,' she told me."

"So I'm one of her patients, too, I guess."

"She can't help healing everybody in sight. Born that way, I guess. If only she could heal herself." Ree Meh sighs. "She's so good it's hard sometimes. I can never catch up. Good night, Tu Reh."

She climbs up a couple of rungs, but I grab the hem of her sarong before she can disappear. "I like a girl who isn't perfect," I say.

She looks down at me and laughs. "There you go again, Mr. Charming. Are you saying I have flaws?"

"Lots of them," I answer. "So do I. That's why I like you so much."

"Okay, okay," she says. "I get it. Me, too. Now let go of my sarong and go tell Chiko what's happening."

I whistle a love song on the way to the doctor's hut. It's loud, but I don't care who hears me.

25

Chiko is bolt upright in his cot, waiting for me. "Tu Reh! Finally! What did they decide?"

I'm happy I have good news; I can't imagine telling that face that we were going to lug him into the jungle and leave him there. "They're letting you go to the camp to be fitted with a prosthetic. You leave tomorrow."

"They are? I am? But how will I get there?"

"You'll ride my mule. The doctor will clear you at the checkpoint."

He slumps back against the pillows, takes his glasses off, and wipes his eyes. "You . . . you saved my life, Tu Reh. And now you're giving me your mule, too. How can I ever repay you?"

"Tell your people to stop killing Karenni," I say, unrolling my mat to keep my own face out of sight. My voice sounds gruff, but that's only because I don't want to give away what I'm feeling.

"I'll tell everybody in Yangon. You can count on that."

"Good. And Mango's just a loan, mind you."

"I'll take good care of her, I promise."

"Let's get some sleep," I say. "You're leaving early in the morning."

"Good night, Tu Reh."

"Good night, Chiko."

I'm up at dawn, but Auntie Doctor is already getting Chiko ready. We gather to see them off—the grandfather, my sister, the girls, and Mua, who has prepared food for their journey.

"I'll tell my own *mua* what a good cook you are," Chiko tells Mua.

This makes Mua happy. "She will be happy to see you," she manages in broken Burmese.

Chiko hands me the books he's been reading nonstop while he's been recovering. "Could you please return these to your teacher? I loved them. They made me forget everything for a while. And when I was finished, I had just enough courage to face—to see—to go home like this." He gestures to his stump.

"Your family will be grateful to see you alive," the grandfather says. "Those who love you will receive you just as you are."

Chiko doesn't look convinced, but he takes the grandfather's outstretched hand. "Thank you," he says. "I'll never forget you."

"Go in peace, my boy," says the grandfather.

Ree Meh, Nya Meh, and I manage to get Chiko on Mango without jarring his injured leg. He sits there precariously, looking a bit uneasy.

"I'm out of balance without my shin and foot," he tells Nya Meh. "Sometimes it feels like I still have them. I keep having to touch my stump to remember that they're no longer there."

"They'll fit you with a good replacement," she says. "You'll be walking again in no time."

"I'll call that one my Karenni leg," he tells us. "It's going to prove to everybody how good you've been to me."

We walk slowly to the river, leaving the grandfather, Mua, and my sister behind. Chiko *is* unsteady up on Mango—several times he has to clutch her mane or one of our shoulders to keep his seat.

"Wait," I say after he's grabbed me for the fourth time. We're near the river now, so the bamboo is close by. I take my knife from my belt and cut a long piece of it, almost the same length as the one I usually carry.

Chiko takes it and leans his weight on it every now

and then as Mango carries him to the gate. "It's perfect," he says.

"I'll be back soon to do some more training," Auntie Doctor tells Nya Meh. "In the meantime, read that medical book I left behind. And I'll keep this animal safe, Tu Reh. I promise."

"Thank you, Auntie." Nya Meh looks up at Chiko with a smile. "Be well, my brother."

"Thanks to you, I will," he replies.

"Good-bye, Chiko," adds Ree Meh.

"Take care of Tu Reh," he tells her, and grins at me.

And then it's my turn. How strange that it's hard to say good-bye.

"I hope we see each other again, Tu Reh," Chiko tells me, clasping my hand tightly.

"I hope so, too. God be with you, Chiko."

"Good-bye, my brother," he replies, leaving me with a gift of three words, all in Karenni.

26

Auntie Doctor was right; life settles down in camp after Chiko leaves. Even though we don't have Mango to help, the work on the girls' hut moves quickly. I keep an anxious eye on the sandy shore across the river. Peh and the team should be returning soon.

The taller bamboo is on the far side of the river, so Ree Meh and I have to cross it to cut the few pieces we need. We're smack in the middle of the water when we see Sa Reh and the healer, wading side by side in the shallows.

Ree Meh and I are in the deepest part of the

river, the current swirling around our waists, when Nya Meh turns and comes toward us. She's moving fast, as though she wants to get away from Sa Reh, but Sa Reh follows her.

"I've been trying to convince your sister to keep away from this traitor," Sa Reh says to Ree Meh once they reach us. "This coward won't protect you. The Burmese will take you, and he'll stand by and do nothing."

Ree Meh lifts her chin. "I can protect myself," she says. "And Tu Reh isn't the only one who saved that boy's life. My sister did her part as well."

"Your sister's a healer," Sa Reh says, his voice getting louder. "She had no choice. But your boyfriend is a Karenni man. He should have killed that soldier."

I couldn't let Ree Meh keep fighting my battles with Sa Reh. "I won't let anybody else decide when it's my time to kill," I tell him. "Or even to fight. A Karenni man chooses for himself."

Once again Sa Reh's fists are clenched. "Are you preaching to me? I'm telling you to stay away from these girls."

"I won't! I told Peh I'd protect them, and I'm going to keep doing it!"

"*I'll* protect them from now on—not you!"

With a roar, he lunges toward me. His big hands grasp me and push me into the water. I try to twist away, but he's bigger and angrier than I am. He's trying to hold my head under the water, but I manage to struggle out of his grasp.

I catch my balance, panting for air. "What do you want from me?" I shout. "I did what I thought was right. It *was* right. I'd do it again."

"Traitor!" Sa Reh yells, coming at me again, angry as the wild bull elephant in the jungle.

I brace myself to meet him.

A voice rings out: "Stop!"

It's Nya Meh, and for the first time since I've met her, her tone is harsh.

Sa Reh obeys. So do I.

Again and again the word rings out, like the warning screech of a crow: "Stop! Stop!" But Nya Meh herself can't seem to stop. She covers her face with her hands, begging us to stop, over and over again, until at last her voice dwindles to a broken whisper.

Ree Meh holds her close. Then Nya Meh says something in a low voice to her sister. Ree Meh looks up angrily. "She says you sounded just like they did when they used to fight over her."

Sa Reh flinches as if the words have slapped him.

I look down at the water to hide my shame.

Nya Meh's body is shaking like bamboo in a storm. "Come, sister," Ree Meh says, and she helps Nya Meh to shore. They head for our hut, their wet sarongs making them move slowly.

With a low groan, Sa Reh turns and begins splashing up the river, disappearing around the bend. Slowly I walk home.

Ree Meh stops me at the bottom of the ladder. "Your *mua* is taking care of her, Tu Reh," she tells me. "You can't come up."

"Are you angry at me?" I ask.

She shakes her head. "No. Just sad for my sister. But this is needed."

She climbs back up, and I stay at the foot of the ladder as it grows dark, listening to Nya Meh's low, trembling voice speak, fall silent, and then speak again. I can't make out the words. This must be the confession that Ree Meh's been hoping for, but I'm not sure either sister can bear it. I can hardly believe that Sa Reh and I have brought it about with our ugly fight.

After a while I leave and make my way to the site of the girls' new hut. It's almost done, but the place still needs a door and some windows. I slash bamboo in the last light of dusk and drag the branches to the hut as the full moon rises over the hills. I work for an hour or so, cutting, fitting, and tying bamboo to make a door.

As I'm struggling to lift it, I hear someone approaching, and then Sa Reh is beside me. He puts his strong shoulder next to mine, and together we manage to heave the door into place.

"Couldn't have done it alone," I say.

"Sorry I spit at you," he says. His voice is so low and gruff I can barely make out the words, but I do.

"You've got to quit that betel nut habit," I say. "Girls don't like it."

"I know. I'll try."

We frame the windows through the rest of the night without saying much more, handing each other pieces of bamboo, rope, and tools. We finish before dawn and rest on a low rise behind the hut, admiring our work. The door and window frames fit snugly, but the hut still needs to be weatherproofed for the rainy season.

Sa Reh hands me half a banana. "Is she okay?" he asks.

"I hope so. I think so. She never talked about what happened. Not until now."

"She . . . she doesn't hate them."

"I know."

"She saved that soldier's life."

I pop the last piece of banana into my mouth, relishing the sensation of Sa Reh's easy company—something I thought I'd lost forever. "She called him 'my brother.'"

"I like her," he says. "I—I wish I were half as good as she is."

"Who doesn't?"

The air is still; the roosters are beginning to sing. The first light lines the dark hills with gold.

"Tu Reh, look!" my friend says, pointing across the river.

On the far bank, coming down the trail where I'd carried Chiko, are four men. Their leader plods wearily in front, but he holds his head high as he reaches the sandy shore.

I recognize him immediately.

"Peh!" I leap to my feet.

Sa Reh and I race to the shore on this side, my heart soaring. The sun sparkles across the valley and the roosters sing in chorus.

Peh is splashing through the water—he sees me, and his smile is brighter than the sun.

There's so much to tell, so much to hear.

I stand proudly on this side of the river, waiting for Peh to join me.

EPILOGUE

CHIKO

A rickshaw carries me home. My heart starts beating faster as we get closer. Mother doesn't know I'm coming—there has been no way to get the news of my discharge to her before my arrival.

I know she'll embrace me, leg or no leg, just as the old Karenni man told me. But how will Lei like watching me shuffle around? Will my new leg be repulsive to her? Sometimes it is to me. When I take off the prosthetic to wash my stump, I have to choke back my disgust. I'm not always successful; I've lost even more weight, thanks to the limited amount of food I manage to keep in my stomach.

As the house comes into sight, I try to remember Frodo from *The Lord of the Rings*, who lost a finger on his journey. *No hero comes back unscarred*, I remind myself. I'm still the same Chiko inside even though I'm stick-thin and disfigured—I'll have to convince Lei of that. But somehow I'll have to believe it first myself.

I hitch up my *longyi* a bit so they'll see my leg right away and I can get the bad news over with fast.

The rickshaw stops in front of the familiar house. "I'll be back with the fare," I tell the driver.

Why didn't I run more with my feet when I had both of them? I should have sprinted, jumped, leaped, danced, skipped, bounded here and there like a rabbit. Now I limp slowly to the door, but it flies open before I reach the threshold. And Mother is with me in the path; she's crying hard and holding tight to my arm.

"You're so thin, Chiko!" she says when she can finally speak. "I can't wait to start feeding you again."

What? I've lost my leg, and all she can think about is food? Maybe she hasn't noticed. "They made me a new one, Mother," I say, pointing to it.

"I know, my son, I know," she says. And then, to my amazement, she tosses her standards of appropriate behavior aside and stoops to kiss my Karenni leg, right in front of the gaping rickshaw driver.

The door flies open again, and I can't believe my

eyes. Because Tai runs out of the house—our house—and hurries past us to pay the rickshaw driver.

Mother, embarrassed over her show of affection, gets up. "Don't tell Chiko *anything* until we're all inside, Tai!" she calls, and disappears into the house. I figure she's probably headed straight to the kitchen to start boiling rice.

Once the driver is satisfied with his fare, Tai races back to clasp my hands and gives me that familiar grin. But it fades as he catches sight of my injury.

"Oh, no!" he says. "Your leg, Chiko! Your leg!"

"It got me home," I say.

"But it should have been me. Not you."

"Don't be an idiot," I say. "I don't have a sister to protect. Where is she, anyway?"

"Inside, because your mother asked us to stay here," he tells me as we walk to the door. He moves slowly to match my pace.

"I told you she would," I say as we walk inside. "So what's the big news?"

"I can't say anything until we're all in the room," Tai says. "Your mother will want to see your face."

"I'm just putting the rice on," Mother calls from the kitchen, making me smile at how well I can predict her actions. "I'll be there in a minute!"

I'm curious, but I'm so glad to be home that I don't mind waiting for whatever the big announcement is. Everything in the house looks the same, from the white elephant on the wall to the table and chairs set for dinner. Sawati comes in carrying an extra plate, and she, too, stops to stare at my leg. "Can I touch it?" she asks.

"Certainly," I say.

She puts the plate on the table and raps the prosthetic with her knuckles. "Hard as a rock," she says. "If you kick someone in the head with this thing, you'll kill them."

We laugh, and Tai seems to relax. Now Mother's there, too, handing me a glass of juice. "Quiet, Sawati," Tai says. "I have to tell Chiko something. I'm working at army headquarters now, and you'll never believe this, but—"

The front door flies open again. It's Daw Widow, of course, coming to inspect the commotion. She sees me and stops, tears coming to her eyes—it's the first time I've ever seen her cry. Even more amazing is that for once she doesn't seem to be able to say anything. Daw Widow, speechless? This is truly a day to remember. Mother rushes to her side, and they cry together.

And then I catch my breath. Lei, the sparkling, colorful, *real-life* Lei, comes into the house, looking more beautiful than ever. Her eyes travel down to my leg and back up to my face, but she's smiling, happy tears in her eyes, too, not a shred of disgust in sight.

"You're home, Chiko," she says. "I'm so glad."

Daw Widow wipes her face and takes a deep breath. "Tai told us how brave you were," she says. "Well done, boy. I knew you had it in you."

"My leg—" I start again. Why doesn't Daw Widow see it? Why do I have to be the one to point it out?

"I know, I know," Daw Widow says. "Noticed it right when I came in. It's not bad. Rubber, metal, and plastic, right? Who made it?"

They *don't* care about the leg. The old man was right. "The Karenni. They saved my life." If I want to keep my promise to Tu Reh and let all of Yangon know, telling Daw Widow is a good place to start.

She turns to Tai. "Did you tell him the news?" she asks.

"I tried," Tai says. "I've been trying."

"Well, tell him now, boy," Daw Widow says. "It's all your doing, anyway."

Suddenly everybody's talking at once. At first I can't understand anything they're saying. Then I hear Mother's voice, chiming like a temple bell above the others. "Your father—he's coming home, Chiko!"

"What?" I can't have heard right, can I?

Again they answer at the same time, making my head spin as I turn from one person to the other.

"Tai found out where he was—"

"I went to see him right away—"

"He was so ill, Daw Widow convinced them—"

"He'll be released in a month, Chiko. A month!"

I don't say anything. I can't. Instead I take my precious photos out of my pocket.

"You kept those safe all this time?" Daw Widow asks.

The flesh-and-blood Lei is here now with a face full of love. I hand her photo back to Daw Widow. "Thank you so much for that," I say. "But I prefer the real version."

Daw Widow and Mother exchange significant looks as Lei smiles at me.

I'll keep the other photo until Father gets home. His image sustained me through everything I endured. I gaze at it again, remembering how Tu Reh said he saw the same expression on my face.

I glance quickly at my reflection in the glass of the white elephant picture.

He was right.

I see it now, too.

ABOUT MODERN
BURMA

Slightly smaller than Texas in size, the country of
Burma shares borders with India, Laos, China,
Bangladesh, Thailand, and the Bay of Bengal. It's
a land of diversity, with over one hundred lan-
guages, several religions, fertile plains, and rugged
highlands. The country was once described as the
"rice bowl of Asia" and enjoyed one of the high-
est literacy rates in Southeast Asia.

Sadly that didn't last. Today about ninety percent of Burma's people live at or below the poverty
line, and the country's health system is ranked
second worst in the world. About ten percent of

children die before the age of five, and the literacy rate has been plummeting each year.

How did the region's "rice bowl" become a place of suffering, disease, and hunger? It's a sad story of injustice and corruption.

Once ruled by Britain, Burma became an independent parliamentary democracy in 1948. Ethnic groups like the Shan, the Karen, and the Wa wanted to keep their independence and avoid being controlled by the Burmese majority. Despite tension and strife, the country survived as a representative government for fourteen years. In 1962, however, military leaders staged a coup and took control of the country.

Things went from bad to worse—the army shut down free elections, took over newspapers and businesses, and clamped down on freedom of expression, association, and assembly. People tried to resist, but the military brutally crushed student and worker demonstrations in the 1960s and 1970s. The government tortured and imprisoned anyone brave enough to speak out. At the same time, ethnic groups along the country's frontiers continued to struggle for independence. To fight these "insurgents," as they were labeled, the government began forcing young Burmese men into the army.

On the eighth of August, 1988 (8/8/88), hundreds of thousands of people gathered peacefully and demanded that the military regime step down in favor of an elected civilian government. But the nonviolent protest didn't work. Soldiers opened fire on unarmed marchers, killing thousands, and arrested and tortured thousands more.

Aung San Suu Kyi, daughter of one of the first leaders of Burma who had been killed in 1947, helped to form a political party called National League for Democracy (NLD). The military government put her under house arrest in 1989 and threw many of the top senior NLD officials in prison. Even when the people voted resoundingly for Suu Kyi and the NLD in a 1990 election, the military refused to step down and seat the new leaders.

The government has only become more repressive since then. When Cyclone Nargis hit Burma in May 2008, the government initially blocked international aid and put more people in jail without just cause. By the end of 2009, the total number of political prisoners in Burma was over two thousand.

The military makes money by controlling industries like mining, logging, oil, transport, manufacturing, apparel, and electricity, and by regulating exports and foreign investment. What happens to all that income? Half is spent on the military and next to nothing on health care and education. And the rulers are lining their own pockets, of course. While the elite live in luxury, the vast majority of Burmese don't know if they'll be able to feed their families tomorrow.

As for the ethnic groups, the army tortures and kills

minorities, uses them for hard labor, and burns their villages. Thousands of people hide in the jungle as internally displaced people, while some flee across the border to Thailand to seek shelter in refugee camps. About one hundred forty thousand refugees live in nine camps along the Thai-Burma border. Since 2004, over fifty thousand refugees representing different minority groups in Burma have been resettled in other countries such as the United States, Canada, Australia, and Norway. The Karenni, however, were not allowed into the United States until 2009. At the time of this writing, the situation for the majority of Karenni still in Burma or Thailand remains grim.

AUTHOR'S NOTE

For three years my husband, children, and I lived in Chiang Mai, Thailand. While we were there we visited the Karenni refugee camps along the Thai-Burma border. I was astounded at how the Karenni kept their hopes up despite incredible loss, still dreaming and talking of the day when they would once again become a free people. I was impressed, too, by how creatively the Karenni used bamboo. Homes, bridges, transportation, weapons, food, storage, irrigation—all these and more depended on the resilient and ecologically efficient bamboo plant. I began to think about that plant as an excellent symbol for the peoples of that region.

During that time I also began to understand how tough life is for Burmese teenagers. Only about a third are enrolled in school, and most can't find jobs. According to international human rights organizations, Burma has the largest number of child soldiers in the world, and that number is growing. These young soldiers are taught that the Karenni and other ethnic groups are the cause of the problems in their country, and they are rewarded with money and food if they burn, destroy, torture, and kill ethnic minorities.

In my travels far and wide, I've learned that all people feel powerful negative emotions, and we all face choices when it comes to acting on them.

What would you do if your mother was hungry and your only option to feed her was to fight in the army? What if you saw soldiers burning your home and farm while you ran for your life? Wouldn't you be terrified, like Chiko? Wouldn't you be angry, like Tu Reh?

I hope you connect with Tu Reh and Chiko as you read *Bamboo People*. If you want to promote peace and democracy in Burma or help refugees fleeing from that country, please visit **www.bamboopeople.org,** where I provide resources, a teacher's guide, and suggestions for involvement.

WHAT'S IN A NAME?

You may not find the country of Burma listed in some books printed after 1989. That year the military government changed the country's official English name from "the Union of Burma" to "the Union of Myanmar." Although the United Nations switched to Myanmar, the USA, the UK, and Canada are among the nations that refused to recognize the new name.

As I'm writing this note, newspapers and magazines are also split. *The New York Times, Wall Street Journal*, and CNN use Myanmar, while the *Washington Post* and *Time* use Burma. For *Bamboo People* I chose to use Burma because that's what the Burmese people use in informal, everyday conversation, reserving the use of Myanmar for formal and ceremonial speech.

ACKNOWLEDGMENTS

Our friends David Eubank, Karen Eubank, Hte Reh, and Hte Mar took me into the refugee camps, translated my questions, read drafts of the novel, and gave suggestions and feedback. You are my heroes.

My critique group in Newton greatly helped to shape this book. Both my agent, Laura Rennert, and my publisher, Charlesbridge, deserve their reputations for championing stories about marginalized voices. Editor Yolanda LeRoy was flexible, creative, and insightful as she shepherded this project to the finish line. I'm proud to work with all of you.

As always, I owe thanks to my parents. Despite the loss of their childhood homes in Bengal, they embarked on a fresh start here in the United States for the sake of my sisters and me. I'm grateful for my sons, who listened to me read several versions of the book and responded with patience and truth. And I wouldn't have lived in Thailand if it weren't for my husband, an excellent companion in the adventure of following Jesus.

Last but not least, I acknowledge the brave men and women who sacrificed and continue to sacrifice so much in their fight for a free Burma, including Daw Aung San Suu Kyi. Let justice roll down in that land.